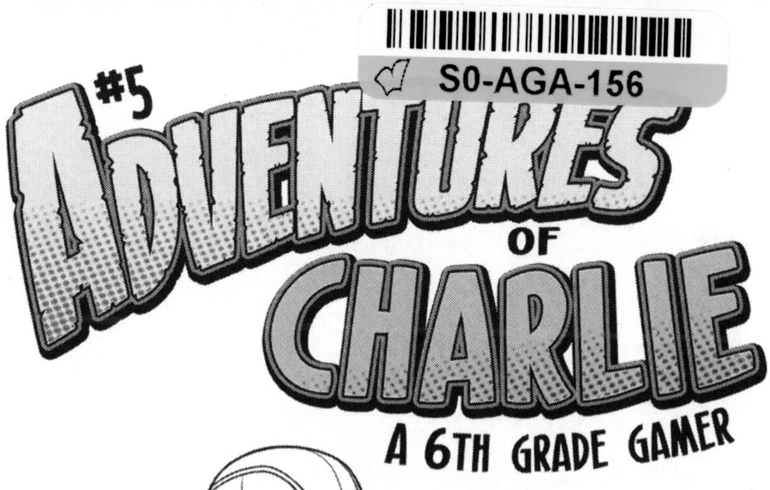

WRITTEN BY

CONNOR GRAYSON

< P.S.- DON'T FEED THE DRAGONS >

The locked tube isn't really a tube. It's a trap.

Of course, I didn't know this when I slipped inside. I do now because I'm stuck.

It's a small, gnome-sized black box. At least, I imagine it's gnome-sized. I mean, the guy who came out of the tube fit in here with room to spare, and he was a gnome. At least, I think he was a gnome, although, he didn't have a pointy red hat.

I'm sitting cross-legged with my head bowed so much I'm staring at my belly button. Definitely too big. There's a crick in my neck. It's so dark, I can't see anything.

What did I get myself into? Maybe I can still take Wizard's deal and go home? I reach my hands out and find the wall. It's metallic and cold.

"Wizard?" I whisper into the darkness.

Nothing.

I punch the wall, *bang*, and vibrations sprint up my arm. "Hello!"

Nothing.

"Anyone!" I yell, flexing my fingers to massage away the tingly sensation. Leaning back, my elbows slam the wall behind me, *bang, bang*, and my mind reels.

What if I'm stuck here forever? I'll never see my friends again. Or my mom. Never play another video game.

My heart creeps into my throat and I swallow hard.

Focus, Charlie. Take a deep breath. You can do this. This is a game. It's only a game. There's a way out. There's always a way out, you just need to find it.

Closing my eyes, I reach out and gently slide my hands over the walls. There's a texture to the metal, like a billion tiny tentacles teasing my palms.

Scooting up onto my knees, I run my hands along

the floor. "I know it's here. It has to be," I say, exploring the corners of the box with my fingertips. "Can I just fast-forward to the next level?"

I really wish this part of the game was over. Reaching up to push on the metal ceiling, I feel it. There it is!

A keyhole?

It's square and round at the same time. I poke my finger inside and wiggle it around. It's full of sharp teeth.

Definitely a keyhole.

I squint and concentrate on Goober's keys. I have a feeling I know which key to use.

ZOOP!

The keyring pops to the top of my bottomless jeans pocket. Remember that? It's the coolest thing I have. It never gets full, no matter how much junk you stuff in there. The trick is remembering what's inside.

The keys poke out of my pocket and I slip them out. I flip past the tube key, past the nasty mini toothbrush, and find the skeleton key.

Run your fingers along the haft and feel the letters engraved there. See them in your mind's eye. *Property of The Clockwork King*.

It's the master key, and it's going to get me out of this box. I'm sure of it.

Using my fingers, I guide the skeleton key into the

keyhole. It slides in easily. I take a deep breath, hold it for the count of three, and then let it slip out.

"Here goes," I say, and twist the key.

CLUNK!

"AHH!" I scream, squeezing my eyes closed tight as everything explodes in light. Music starts to play. Cheesy music, like from one of my Dad's old video games—the gamer's equivalent of elevator music.

I spin around and bang my head. Ow! Cracking an eye open, I peek around. Letters dance across the walls like someone is typing a message on a computer screen.

<Doing something you don't want to know.>

"What the..." I say, not sure what to think.

<Don't worry, this will only take a second.>

"What will take only a second? Who are you?"

<You might want to hold on to something.>

"Wait, what?"

<Don't feed the dragons or else!>

"Dragons? What—" I start to say, but the bright light fades and the music dies.

<LOADING PLEASE WAIT.>

Then the world drops out from under me.

"AHH!" I scream as my stomach flips a thousand times and I free-fall into who knows what.

GOOBER'S BROTHER

I slam into a cold, metal floor. Sound explodes all around me. The *clang, clang, bang, bang* of metal on metal. The *brrrrrrrrrrrrrrrrrrr* of saws on steel. Pushing myself up, I peer around. Everything's blurry, and it's like bees are buzzing around in my head.

"King!" A voice bellows from behind me, it's deep and low like a bear. "King, get back! Out of the line of fire!"

"What?" I squeak out and spin around, searching for the voice. They are yelling at me, right? There's a quick shuffle of feet, along with a *clank, clank*, before a strong, icy hand grips my collar and yanks me across the floor. Skidding to a stop behind a massive pile of... I slap my hand over my nose. "Ugh, what's that smell?"

"Gym shorts, sir. Breathe through your mouth," the bearish mystery man says. I turn towards the voice, but there's nothing but a blurry, blob head.

I close my eyes, shake my head, and swallow hard. Don't gag. When I open my eyes, staring back at me is someone I know.

"Goober?"

"Name's Brendon. I'm Goober's twin brother," he says, holding out a hand. I reach out to shake and then just stare. The silver hand in front of me isn't a real hand, rather, it's a robot hand straight out of a sci-fi movie. It's attached to a robot arm coming out of a heavy tool belt wrapped around Brendon's waist.

"AHH!" I scurry back as fast as I can, but my feet slip and slide on the metal floor.

"Easy, easy. It's just another tool in the belt," he says, pulling out other tools on his belt and holding them up for me to inspect. Not hammers or wrenches, but rather hooked screwdrivers, twirly bird springs, and other things that make no sense.

Each time he holds up a tool, my Wizard Eyes light up—icons flashing in the corner of my vision. That's new. What do they mean?

Brendon is wearing a jumper, and like Goober, it covers even his hands and feet. Well one foot. The other has a metal shoe thing on it. On his chest is a name tag for Brendon, but it was spelled wrong, so he taped a big E on it. Brendon, not Brandon.

There are a few other patches on his jumper. I think they're made of metal too. Is it armor? A greasy worker's cap loosely sits on his big head. Think baseball cap, but without the bill in front. There's a big B in the center, written in crayon.

"What is—" I start to say, and then his robot hands darts out and yanks me so close I smell his breakfast. Dead fish. Ugh. Definitely Goober's brother.

"Where's King? Why do you have his gear? Who are you? Why are you here?"

"Let go," I say, squirming to get free of his grip.

Brendon lets me go and huffs. "Relax. I'm not going to hurt you. Who are you?"

"My name's Charlie." I sit back and cross my arms across my chest. "I'm a gamer."

"Good, good," he says as he pulls a very long, very pointing tool out of his tool belt. "And why are you here?"

"I need to find The Chef." Brendon busts up

laughing and I pause. My face gets hot, and I glare at Goober's twin before continuing. "At least that's what Young Lady Fate said I need to do."

"You know Young Lady Fate? How?"

"That's a long story…"

Brendon waves it away. "Doesn't matter. I can take you to The Chef, but first answer my questions. What'd you do with King? Why are you wearing his gear?"

I look down and flip my hands over, inspecting the gauntlets the gnome from the locked tube gave me. That was King? Rubbing my chainmail vest with a hand, I wonder why I'm wearing this stuff. Is it going to help me beat Wizard? What am I supposed to do now? Find The Chef and recruit an army? That's all he said.

Is there even a boss mob to beat in this level? My heart aches. I really wish I could talk to my friends. I squeeze my eyes closed and whisper to myself. "I don't know…"

"Hello, Charlie," Brendon says, knocking on my leather skullcap. "Anyone home?"

I let the thoughts drift away, and snap my eyes open. Brendon's staring back at me, a goofy Goober grin on his face. "He said I need The Chef and an army if I'm ever going to beat Wizard." I wave my hands at the gear I'm wearing. "This is supposed to convince the gnomes I'm him. I guess."

Brendon dives forward and tackles me to the ground. Slamming his forearm under my chin, he glares at me. "Think before you answer this next question. It'll decide what I do with you."

"Do with me?" I squeak out.

"Either I'll help you on your quest or I'll toss you into the endless tube." My eyes bulge as Brendon presses down on my throat ever so slightly. "What is the password? If you don't know it, I'll know you're a liar."

Password? Do I have a password? I rack my brain trying to remember.

"EGGPLANTS!" I blurt out, and Brendon slaps a rough hand over my mouth.

"Shh!" He hisses, whipping his head side to side nervously. "Someone may be listening."

As he relaxes his hold on me, I scoot back and rub my throat. "Are you going to take me to The Chef?"

Brendon narrows his eyes at me for like forever and finally says, "Maybe. It seems you're supposed to be here, but you're going to have to prove it."

"Prove it? How?"

Brendon points over my shoulder. "Free the red dog."

RED DOG

I poke my head around the mountain of dirty laundry and peer into the room Brendon's pointing at.

"Whoa."

It's a huge open floor like an airplane hangar. Two dozen planes could fit in here! The brick walls are reinforced with metal beams. In the center of the wall, furthest from me, is a massive golden door glittering with ivory dials. It reminds me of the golden door with seven locks in the Nexus.

Sitting in front of the door is a massive throne, covered in purple velvet. Looks super comfy. In the seat is a miniature, bright red dodgeball, about the size of a baseball. What's that for?

Splitting the room in half is a bright white line. It's about as wide as my hand. On either side, a big circle is drawn on the floor with the same bright white paint as the center line. Or is it chalk? I don't know.

On the left side of the room, angry robots snarl and snap jaws of steel as tiny gnomes zip around waving Brendon-style tools in the air.

Ugly, green trolls roam this way and that on the other side of the room. Like they're waiting for a game to start. It's weird.

"What's going on?"

"It's the never-ending war," Brendon says, and as I turn back to him, he shrugs.

"Never ending? There's not much fighting going on."

"They can't exactly get to each other, but they die trying." Brendon chuckles. I raise an eyebrow, not quite sure what he means.

"What are they trying to win?"

"No one knows, but the poor pup is stuck in the

middle of the fight." Brendon frowns, slowly shuffling his feet.

I scan the hanger, searching for the red dog. It's like an odd game of *Where's Waldo*. A group of humanoid robots form a big pyramid on their side of the big purple throne like a bunch of cheerleaders. Hiding behind them is a Clifford-sized dogbot, steam gushing out of its nostrils. Light gleaming off the various blades fixed to his body. Farther back is what looks like an auto shop. Gnome engineers repair robots with their weird tools, and orange-red sparks splash across the metal floor, only to die seconds later.

A pack of beanpole troll warriors show off by spinning curved swords at their sides like airplane propellers. They have red sashes tied around their foreheads and massive tusks like an elephant. Their brown pants are caked in dirt, and in the center of their t-shirts is the image of a dodgeball.

"Where's the red dog?"

"Do you have the whistle? King always blew the whistle, and he'd come bounding out."

The whistle! I yank it out of my shirt and inspect the silver metal. It looks like a normal whistle. Pressing it to my lips, I blow, and unlike the ghost dog's whistle, it roars to life.

FWEET!

Every monster in the room freezes, then whips

toward me! I glance at Brendon and widen my eyes with a *what did I just do* question plastered on my face. He snatches a tiny telescope out of his tool belt and starts scanning the room. “Quick, find the red dog. They’re coming!”

“Who’s coming?” Turning back, my question is answered when every gnome, robot, and troll sprints toward me.

“There! Under the throne. Go,” Brendon says, shoving me towards the angry mob of monsters.

“Wait, what?” My eyes snap to the throne, and peeking out from underneath are two scared eyes. The red dog. “How am I going to get—”

“Go get him. I’ll meet you at Wendell’s.” Brendon slams a button on his tool belt and disappears. He’s just… gone. His foot goes *clank, clank, clank* as he sprints away, yelling, “Bring the red dog. Prove yourself!”

Whipping back towards the monsters, I have about two seconds before I’m lunch. Which way to go? Straight ahead is the throne. On the left—gnomes and their angry robots. On the right—ugly, green trolls with swords.

Think, Charlie. Think!

I bolt to the left. Robots and gnomes with tiny legs must be slower than trolls, right?

WOOF! WOOF!

The humongous dogbot bounds to the front of the robot mob, slamming down and blocking my path. Pivoting back to center, I dart towards the troll army. They're snarling and shuffling down the white line in the center of the room. One of the sword warriors raises his wicked, curved blade and lashes forward.

CLANG!

Skidding to a stop, I glance at the sword that's stuck in midair. "What the…" The warrior yanks with all his might to free the sword from *something*.

The big, ugly green monster snarls and drops the stuck sword. Bearing back, he shakes his fists at me, then drops a shoulder and dives. He's bum-rushing me—using his body as a battering ram! I squeeze my eyes shut, cringe, and wait for impact…

Waiting…

Waiting…

THUD!

Cracking my eyes open, the fighter's nose is smooshed to the side like he ran into a wall. I glance down and there's the white line dividing the room. Does it mark an invisible wall? Following the line, it leads right to the throne.

Hmm, I wonder.

Turning around, I face the robots still coming for me. "Hey big ugly! I bet you wish you were a real dog!" If this goes sour, I'll be dog food.

The dogbot growls and lowers his massive spiked head. There's a *whir* and his entire body shimmers red, before he lunges forward so fast his body blurs.

This could be bad.

Bouncing on the balls of my feet, I hold steady until the dogbot's steam breath is hot on my face, then dive across the barrier to the troll side.

CRUNCH!

The dogbot slams the invisible wall so hard, his snout crunches and screams like a crumpled soda can. The robot army tries to stop behind him, but slide across the slick, metal floor and *crunch* right into the dogbot's butt! Gnome engineers start screaming about broken bits, and the *clang, clang* of tools hitting metal vibrates the air.

"Ha! Nice," I shout, and start laughing before I hear snarling to my right. Trolls! I push myself up and sprint away from the pack of angry trolls.

How wide is the invisible wall? I mean, there's the white line, but is the barrier bigger? It separates the robots from the trolls, that's obvious, but is it wide enough for me to run down the center safe from *all* monsters? Or must I bounce side-to-side in a dangerous game of can't catch me?

BARK!

I glance over my shoulder and spot the red dog.

He's on top of the throne, instead of under it. "What is it, boy?" I yell, hoping he'll clue me in.

BARK! BARK!

He scratches at the throne's seat. Purple velvet and stuffing fly into the air. What's he doing?

Back where I started, I swing around the mountain of yesterday's sweaty gym socks and notice robots putting themselves back together—they'll be back in the fight in seconds. The trolls barrel straight for me.

I'll have to figure it out on the fly. There's no time.

Bolting towards the trolls, I squeeze my hands into fists and pump my legs hard. A second before I'm lunch, I leap to the left, crossing into robot territory. By instinct, the lead troll lunges for me and slams into the wall. Losing his balance, he tumbles to the ground, spinning away, taking a few of his friends with him.

Yes! It's going to work.

CLANG! CLANG!

The robots are moving again. Those gnomes fix things fast! They're gaining ground on me from behind, plus there's a second group up ahead—forming a blockade. Smart gnomes and big robots equal a bad combo.

My guts grumble and a groan slips out. New plan.

"Take them out," I whisper to myself. "Maybe a little boom, boom." A burp from deep in my belly explodes from my mouth, along with a stream of black magic. Flies to the rescue!

My breath is heavy and my nose burns. Keep running. You've got to keep running. My magic forms a massive fist and races for the robots like a heat-seeking missile. Glancing behind me, I check for trolls. There's a new pack gaining on me. These have battle hammers! You'll never win if you don't risk it all.

I vault over the center line and through the barrier, landing in troll territory. I sprint as hard as I ever have and explode forward. Keep out of smashing range!

BOOM!

My magic fist pummels the robots and parts explode in every direction. I cringe as an arm slams into the barrier right next to my head. Whew. Thank you, invisible wall thing. Hopping back to robot land, it's clear to the throne.

I skid to a stop and the red dog turns towards me. He grins, white and purple cushion pieces flump from his mouth to the floor with a wet *smack*.

"Johnson! It is you!" I yell, getting goosebumps all over. "But you're not the ghost dog." My mind reels. How is that possible?

The red dog hops on the throne, knocking the miniature red dodgeball off, and digs into the seat with his front paws. I ignore the flying stuffing and snatch up the dodgeball. It's glowing. I inspect it with my

Wizard Eyes. There's a short message that says, *Unique item. This may come in handy.*

I don't know.

Stuffing it into my jean pocket—my bottomless bag—there's a bulge for a second, then it plops to the bottom. It may come in handy later, I guess.

Wandering up to the throne, I peer through the hole in the seat. "It's a tunnel. Do we go in?" I ask the red dog. He barks twice. "I'll take that as a 'sure do.'"

MAGIC ATTACK | MELEE ATTACK

OVERCLOCK

THE DOGBOT IS MEAN AND LEAN, ALWAYS. BUT IF YOU SEE IT TURN RED... RUN! IT'LL CHARGE AND SLAM! IT'LL CHARGE AND SMASH! ITS OVERCLOCK WON'T STOP UNTIL YOU DO! I HOPE YOU'VE BEEN EXERCISING, OTHERWISE, GOOD LUCK!

SMASH

THE DOGBOT IS A SMASH BRO. A TRUE SMASH BRO. IT'LL GAIN SPEED AND MOVE UNTIL IT CAN'T. ALL IN THE NAME OF THE SMASH! THE SMASHING OF YOUR FACE! RUN, RUN, RUN OR YOU'LL BE NOTHING MORE THAN ANOTHER BROKEN BIT IN THE TRASH! HA!

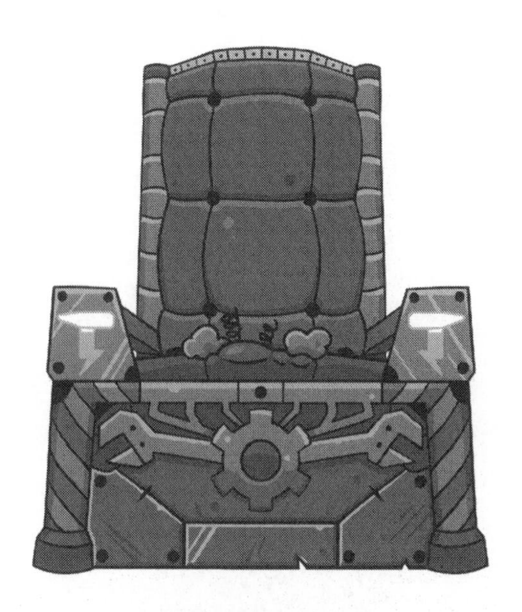

THRONE TUNNEL

★

The red dog flops to his belly and slips through the hole in the throne. The throne is just a big chair sitting on top of a secret passage. Thing is, it's so heavy, there's no way you're going to move it. Trust me, I tried. I'm pretty sure it's bolted to the floor. Either that or lots of gorilla glue.

Stump could probably move it. Man, I miss my friends. I hope they're okay. What do you think they're doing right now? Are they playing the game without me?

I tap my Wizard Eyes twice to turn on night mode, and shove my head into the tunnel. It's tiny, like the black box I started this level in. My heart booms in my ears and my palms are sticky with sweat. "Am I even going to fit?" I ask no one.

The red dog looks up at me from a platform about ten feet down. His tail whips back and forth, clanging into the tunnel wall. He yips at me.

"We need to meet Brendon at Wendell's. Do you know where that is?"

Johnson grins, his tongue flopping out of his mouth, goop dripping on the floor. Two quick barks and he darts to the right, out of sight.

SCRATCH! SCRATCH!

Popping my head out of the secret passage, I spin around and see the dogbot a few feet away, claws raking at the invisible wall. As I stick out my tongue, a gnome engineer wanders up and slams three spikes into the barrier. He attaches a tool to each spike. There's an *ee-ee* sound as the spikes twist and glow red. It's not long before white lines sprint up the wall like cracks in glass.

Not good.

Hopping on the throne, I shove my feet through loose stuffing and wiggle my butt into the hole, careful to not stab myself with a loose metal spring. "Wait for me!" Hugging my arms to my sides, and squeezing my eyes shut, I drop inside.

My head goes *boom, boom* as I slide down smooth metal and finally crash into a small platform. I stand up and shake my head, hoping it doesn't explode. Everything is lime-green from night mode on my goggles. There's a latch on the tunnel wall. A fire alarm? It looks like a fire alarm, minus the word FIRE.

Leaning closer, my Wizard Eyes outline the device with a neon red line. A similar red dot pulsates in the bottom left of my vision. Focusing on the dot, a message flashes in front of me.

Inspect programming of tinkered item 004523?

"Uh, yes?" I remember getting access to the tinkering interface in the fishbowl, but what it is, or how to use it, I have zero idea. Maybe Brendon knows.

Accessing details of details. Please stand by.

Right. Standing by. Looking left, there's another tunnel. I'd need to crawl on hands and knees to go that way. To the right, it's the same. Grr. Soft light and the occasional shadow of movement falls from the hole in the throne above. Have the monster robots broken through the invisible barrier already?

That'd be bad.

Words begin scrolling in my face. I can't see anything but never-ending text, like those terms and conditions you're always supposed to read. Ain't nobody got time for that. Where's the checkbox I can click on?

I catch bits and pieces of a few sentences. Something about protocols, security settings, and failsafes.

I don't know.

At the bottom is a bold line: *User Instructions: Pull the lever to close the throne room hatch.*

Where's the facepalm emoji? Seriously. I pull the fire alarm lever.

PSHH!

I look up, towards the sound, and there's a door sliding closed near the hole in the throne. Nice. No monsters following me down here, but also no turning back.

CLUNK!

Wait, what? The directions only mentioned one hatch. Searching around, everything looks the same. What just clunked? Kneeling, I peek into the tunnel on the left. It's dark, and stinks like socks and sour candy. Weird, but whatever. Spinning around to the right, it's dark and... there's a swooshing sound.

"Johnson! Where are you?"

BARK!

The red dog tears down the right tunnel, his eyes

wide, his fur soaking wet, and a raging tidal wave close behind him.

"AHH!" I yell as the red dog races by. I whirl and race after him in the best, most awkward, bear crawl of my life. The raging waves rumble behind me, nipping at my heels.

Grrblin's voice rings in my head with an *Ohcrapohcrapohcrap*.

FRIENDLY FITZ

I'm lucky there's only one way to go. My brain isn't exactly keeping up with what's happening right now.

"AHH!" I scream, the tidal wave lapping at my feet. Ice-cold water seeps through my shoes and nips at my toes.

BARK!

The red dog's voice—can you call a dog's bark its voice? I don't know. But, Johnson's voice echoes down the metal tunnel. It bounces between the walls, a metal *ting, ting* ringing in my ears. Everything's blurry. My eyes sting from the saltwater in the air. Blinking quickly, I clear them enough to see. Where's the red dog?

On the wall ahead of me is another flashing yellow arrow. It screams to go right. It's the third one I've passed. Maybe fourth. I can't remember. Have they all been to the right? I hope not.

I swing a hard right and bounce off the metal wall with my left shoulder. Up ahead, there's the red dog! Quickly recovering, I scurry on hands and knees as the water slam-splashes behind me. It's only a two-second breather before the wave turns the corner, but it's enough.

CLANG!

A hatch door in the ceiling bangs open between me and the red dog. A head pops out and says, "Dude, what's all the noise?"

The head is like that of a gnome engineer—small round face, and a big, bulbous nose with a long beard to match. A yellow and blue knit hat is pulled over his ears. It's rimmed with an ocean wave and there's a party penguin dancing below the dirty white poof ball at the top. How's it not falling off his head with him hanging from the ceiling—is that a seashell tucked in his beard?

"Incoming!" I yell, barreling down the tunnel, too fast to stop. The gnome's eyes go wide, and he yanks his head back into the hatch right before I zip by.

WHOOSH!

A quick look over my shoulder and I watch half the tidal wave blast through the ceiling hatch with a high-pitched squeal. Run, gnome, run!

Further down the tunnel, the red dog skids to the left and disappears again. I press hard to catch up, barely able to keep up, let alone stay ahead of the wave.

BANG! BANG! BANG!

I glance up towards the banging and imagine what's going on up there. The surfer gnome is sprinting on top of this tunnel. Is it some kind of tube? Does he know where he's going?

CLANG!

Another hatch opens ahead of me and water spits into the tunnel along with the surfer gnome's voice. "Hit the button!"

Button? What button?

The tidal wave growls, a reminder it's coming for me. Get moving, Charlie! I shake the thought of a button from my head and focus. Hand, knee, hand, knee. Crawl. Crawl fast!

CLANG!

Another hatch door and another shout. "Hit the

button! It'll close the—AHH!" The surfer gnome's voice screams, trailing off as the *bang, bang* of his feet take a quick right, leading away from me. He must have hit a dead end and been forced to turn.

I can't shake the thought of a button. What will it close? Quick glances right and left, and I don't see anything. I arrive at the junction where the red dog took a sharp left. It's the same spot the gnome veered to the right. Pivoting and sliding, I tilt left to follow Johnson and as I spin around the corner a pulse of red flashes in my peripheral vision. You know, out of the corner of my eye.

Glancing over my shoulder, a message pops up.

Inspect programming of tinkered item 488934?

I slide to a stop and lean in. Squinting to see through the mist—it's a button! "Yes, inspect. Inspect!"

The roar and crash of the tidal wave bashes into the wall right behind me and shoots up the open hatch.

"Come on, come on."

Accessing details of details. Please stand by.

Oh, no. Not this again. "Hurry, I'm about to get flushed back to the fishbowl!" I shout at the tinkering interface in my Wizard Eyes. At least, I think that's what I'm shouting at. I really don't know.

Text scrolls by and I ignore it.

The wave roars as it slams back down through the

hatch and turns towards me. I suck in a deep breath, plant my feet at the sides of the tunnel, and brace for impact.

OOF!

The wave barrels into me, and it's like I'm stuck inside the body of a huge water snake. I grunt, trying to slice my hand forward to smack the button. Come on, Charlie. Put some muscle into it. My fingers brush the face of the button as the wave strains against me—squeezing me like a mouse. I press harder and *click*.

PSHH!

There's a sound like pressure releasing, and tiny flaps spring open along the tunnel near the floor. As they do, the wave instantly calms and begins to drain away.

Whew.

There's a bang and bark behind me, and I whip around. The red dog is there, soaking wet, but grinning as the surfer gnome rubs his head between the ears.

"Nice dog," he says, grinning himself. "What's his name?"

"Johnson. I think," I say, tilting my head to the side, trying to get water out of my ear. The red dog yips in agreement.

"What kind—"

"Who are you? Why in the world are you down here?" I ask, sloshing forward to meet the gnome.

"Me? I'm Fitz. Down here working on my book."

"Your book? What do you mean?"

"This one dude traveled the world, writing down all his adventures. Even the boring ones. He wrote it all on a single piece of paper! I'm a writer like that dude."

"Wait, what? How is that even possible?"

"It was a really, really long piece of paper. He rolled it up like a beach towel."

"Where's your paper?" I ask. All he's got is sopping wet clothes, a silly hat, and—whoa—big hairy feet like a hobbit.

"I'm playing it smart. I'm writing it digitally, in my head," Fitz says, tapping a finger to the side of his head. "It's all up here and once my adventure is done, I'll write it all down on paper."

"Won't you forget most of it?"

"Nope," he says, lifting his knit hat and flipping it over. Inside is a mess of wires, sprockets, gears, and levers. They're moving back and forth like spiders. "Wendell's got me covered. Sold me this gadget to make sure."

"Did you say Wendell?"

"Right. You know, Wendell's Wares." He waves his hands like it's obvious.

"Can you take me there? Please?" I ask, and the red dog licks Fitz's hand gently.

Fitz smiles at both of us, a sparkle in his eye, and says, "Sure, dude. Let's have an adventure."

Fitz and the red dog head out ahead of me, wandering through the dark tunnel. I follow a few feet behind. Occasionally, Fitz stops, searches the ground, then shrugs and keeps moving forward.

"Which way to Wendell's?"

"Not sure, dude," Fitz says, bending down again, and searching the ground to our right. "The string should be here, but it's gone."

"String? You do know how to get to Wendell's?"

"Sure thing. But I gotta find the string first."

I stop and stare at the happy-go-lucky gnome. Like, really, *really*, stare. "You what?"

"Gotta find the string. I made sure to leave a trail when I went through the maze before. Dude, it was a great idea. I read about it in a book once."

"Maybe would have been a better idea if you could find it, huh?" I ask, facepalming. You can facepalm in real life. It's not just an emoji. "So, help me understand here. The string will lead us to Wendell? Why exactly—"

"The string will get us through the cave maze," Fitz says, crawling further down the tunnel, his nose to the ground. Red dog mimics him, doing the same. "Wendell's is a quick jog from there."

"Cave maze?"

"Ya, it's brutal to get lost in there. The minotaur, the silver spiders, the—"

"Minotaur?"

"Found it!" The easy-going gnome bursts out, jumping to his feet with a long string twirled around his fingers. It's dark green. No wonder he couldn't find it. "Right on pooch. High-five."

The red dog yips and spins circles at Fitz's feet.

I slowly edge closer and tug on the dark green string. Do you think it's like the sticky, green string? Remember how I tied up The Angry Librarian with that? It was magic-strong, and she couldn't get loose. It was awesome. My Wizard Eyes gave me the clue before. Inspecting this new string, there's nothing. Not magical. Sigh.

Tugging again, I follow the string, and it runs right under the wall. Pressing on the wall, it gives a little. "A secret door?"

"You bet, friend. There's always a secret door on an adventure."

CAVE MAZE

☠

I take a deep breath, pause, and wonder what this would be like if it were easy. Then I think about the games I've played on easy-mode.

Boring.

Hard-mode is always more exciting.

"Here goes," I say, pushing the door open as quietly as I can. Hard-mode may be fun, but you gotta play smart.

The other side is exactly what you'd expect, if you were expecting a cave entrance in the side of a mountain and that mountain had enormous horns.

"That's new," Fitz says, head tilted back as he eyes the shiny white horns sticking out of the rock.

Peering into the cave, it's darkish—there are dim lights along each side of the tunnel, along the floor. Like the lights down the aisle of an airplane.

Stepping through the door, I instantly start sweating. Tugging on King's gear, I consider taking the vest of chain mail off, along with the gauntlets. Do I really need them?

Something passes through my legs and I freeze. It tickles like there's a spider crawling up my leg. Holding my breath, I glance down and see Johnson, the red dog, sliding deeper into the tunnel. He turns and grins at me, his eyes glowing an odd purple.

"Follow the string, Charlie-bro," Fitz whispers in my ear. His hand gently presses into my elbow, pushing me forward.

"I am, I am," I say, letting the string trickle through my fingers as I go deeper into the tunnel.

We turn right way too many times and left only so often before we come to a decision point. There's a signpost with flashlight strapped to it, illuminating three signs. Pointing left is *the best way* while right is *the worst way* and straight is *a really terrible way*.

I don't know.

"Why does your string lead down the path for *the worst way*, shouldn't we take *the best way*?"

"No way, man. Think about it. Anything that says it's the best way is a trap. Like, it's a no-brainer, and a really terrible way is a trick. They, like, want you to think that's worse than the worst way. Because, of course, you're going to take the worst way because it's the best way."

"Uh…" I close my eyes and rub the back of my neck. "What?"

"Backwards law, man. Try to float and you'll sink. Let yourself sink and you'll float."

I don't know.

"So, we go the worst way because it's actually the best way, and because the really terrible way isn't actually the worst way."

"Yes. High-five, brother!"

No high-fives, thank you very much.

I glare at Fitz, then follow the string down *the worst way*. Three steps forward and there's a *clomp, clomp, clomp* of hooves on the hard rock floor.

"Freeze," Fitz hisses to me and the red dog. I turn to see him slowly backing up a couple of paces, his eyes wide, sweat dripping down his face.

"What is it?" I whisper, crouching low. The red dog

whines like dogs do and nuzzles his snout into my hand.

The spooked gnome shakes his head and squeezes his eyes closed.

"I smell gnomes!" Something shouts from up ahead. An engine comes to life with a *vroom, vroom,* and the floor shudders. "Tasty, tasty gnomes can't hide from my snout."

"He wasn't here before, wasn't here. Not the best way, definitely the worst. Totally, the worst way," Fitz mumbles, along with more nonsense as he curls into a ball along the cave wall.

"Who is it?" I ask the scared surfer gnome. "Who's coming?"

"It's him. The minotaur."

"Can we run? Where do the other paths go?"

Fitz just shakes his head and curls into a tighter ball. He's shivering like there's a snowstorm in here. There's definitely not, I've got the pit stains to prove it.

"Fitz, I need you. Can we go another way?" I pull Fitz up and force him to look at me.

He stares back for a second, and then his eyes slip side-to-side. I shake him. Squeezing his eyes closed and concentrating, he says, "We'll get lost. No one finds their way through the maze without the string."

Okay. The minotaur. Legendary monster, I know.

Think Charlie, think. What are his powers? In the Percy Jackson book at home, I remember he was fast. Like really, really fast. Did he have a weapon, or just his horns? I can't remember. I'm pretty sure he'll just body-slam you and then spear you through. Percy had to cut off a horn to win.

"Johnson, I have an idea, but I'm going to need your help." The red dog perks up as his name, tilting his head to the side, curious. I start pulling the green string from behind us. I wind it up into a little ball near the wall and cover it in dust, so it looks like a rock.

Fitz pops an eye open and peeks around. "What are you doing?"

"Getting ready to fight the minotaur," I say, reaching into my bottomless jean's pocket.

"With string?"

"Not just with string." I grin and summon Mr. Pointy to the top of my pocket. Remember him? It? Either way, my sword flies into my hand and I yank it out. Calling on my magic, the blade extends—shimmering black like a living shadow. You barely see it, but you can feel the magic.

"What is THAT?" Fitz asks, his eyes popping out of his head.

Grinning, I lean down and whisper my plan in the red dog's ear. His tongue flops out of his mouth, drool dripping on the floor, as he grins. Then he bounds to the string ball and, gently, takes a piece of string in his jaws. Good boy.

VROOM! VROOM! VROOM!

The minotaur turns the corner and I gasp. He's huge! And he's speeding towards us in a go-cart!

Between him and the hunk of moving metal he's riding on, he nearly fills the entire tunnel. He's built like a bodybuilder, with a bull's head and massive curved horns. His chest is bare, if you don't count the endless amount of hair. He's like Mick the Farmer, who, I thought, was as hairy as a wookiee, but I was wrong—he's part minotaur. Sheesh.

"There you are, tasty gnome," the minotaur roars at Fitz. The gnome squeals like a pig and scoots as far back against the wall as he can.

I step towards the monster's right as Johnson slips down the wall to his left with the string. The minotaur ignores us. Okay? He doesn't see anything, except for the tasty gnome snack that is Fitz.

This is great!

Gripping my sword, I pull the magic out of the blade and hold the empty hilt to my side. Small change of plans. I whisper to my black magic flies and say, "I'm going to need a fist. A really, gigantic fist."

VROOM!

The minotaur's go-cart lunges forward, leaving a

black cloud of smoke behind. The engine roars so loud, my teeth rattle. He bends down over the steering wheel, one gigantic fist up in the air like he's getting ready to pop Fitz in the face.

"NOW!" I scream. The monster glances my way for the first time and growls. Out of the corner of my eye, I see the red dog dart past the minotaur. "Fist, fist. Knock him out!"

My black magic swarms between me and the minotaur and transforms into a massive fist. It reminds me of the wrecking ball fist's of the stone reavers in The One-Eye Hag's level.

The minotaur flinches back for a moment, unsure what to do, but then he snarls and yanks the steering wheel hard. The go-cart spins and explodes towards me, right through the magic fist. I dive forward and—

SLAM!

The minotaur cracks into the wall where I just was. Shaking his head, he turns, and before he can come for me again, I yell, "Slam him!" My fist flies across the room and knocks into the giant monster, whose face goes all crunchy before he falls out of the smashed up go-cart.

The red dog dives over the minotaur, the green string tight in his mouth. Then the dog pivots and slips under his head and through his horns, tying up the groaning monster. Johnson is quick as a whip and before long the minotaur is out for the count, just like The Angry Librarian was.

"Hold, hold," I say to no one, hoping the string will be strong enough.

"Race me or..." The minotaur squeezes his fists and slams them to the ground to push himself up. The string creaks against his massive muscles, but doesn't break. The monster's muscles give up, and he crashes to the floor with a *thud*.

"Is he dead?" Fitz says, his voice cracking. "Like, he's not going to eat me, dead?"

"No tasty gnome snacks for the minotaur today." I call my magic back into my sword blade and bound forward with Mr. Pointy. In one quick swipe, I cleave the horn from the minotaur's head, and it tumbles to the ground. The minotaur *poofs* into monster dust, the go-cart going with him.

Johnson snatches up the horn like a bone and trots over to me. I pluck it from his mouth and slip it into my bottomless bag. Who knows when that will come in handy.

"I can't believe it," Fitz says, falling to his back and giggling. "My book will be a bestseller!"

MAGIC ATTACK

BLADES

THE TROLL WARRIOR IS A MASTER OF BLADES. DEEP IN A FIGHT, HE'LL SWING AND SWISH, SPINNING HIS BLADES SO FAST HE MIGHT JUST TAKE FLIGHT! BUT INSTEAD, HE'LL SLICE AND DICE UNTIL YOU'RE FOOD FOR THE MICE. HA! HA!

MELEE ATTACK

BUM-RUSH

A WARRIOR THROUGH AND THROUGH, EVEN DISARMED YOU BETTER WATCH OUT! THIS TROLL WILL BUM-RUSH YOU--USING HIS BODY AS A BATTERING RAM! BE QUICK, OR YOU'LL BE A SPOT ON THE NEAREST WALL! OH, AND BEWARE THE TUSKS! HEHE!

DRAGON EGGS

The dark green string is covered in slobber from the red dog, but I pick it up and slide it through my fingers. The tunnel has been quiet since I defeated the minotaur. No other monsters have popped out of the dark corners, and we've passed quite a few.

"We gotta be close," Fitz says from behind me. I glance back, and he wipes sweat from his face with his knit cap and then slams it back on his head.

“Why do you wear that hat when it’s so hot?” I ask, shaking my head.

“Because it’s styling, dude. Writer’s gotta look good, never know when you’re going to meet a fan.”

I roll my eyes. Right. Fans.

“How close do you think—” I say, and then Johnson blasts past me with a yip. He slides around the bend up ahead. I chase after him, and when I find him, he’s got his snout buried in a shallow hole near the cave wall. The stone floor of the cave has been torn up and there’s lots of dirt full of white speckles.

It reminds me of sand full of tiny seashells. I bend down and take a closer look. The hole might be big enough for the red dog to get through.

“That wasn’t here before,” Fitz says as he huffs and puffs from running to catch up. “I’d remember.”

Getting on my knees, I join Johnson in the dirt. I pick up a handful and let it trickle through my fingers. What are these white things? Rubbing one between my fingers, it disintegrates into a soft powder, making my fingers look like they’re covered in chalk. I sniff my fingers, and it smells like… eggs?

“Eggshells?” I say as I shove my eyeball to the hole in the wall. The red dog licks my face, covering me in slobber. It’s the good kind of gross.

“See anything?” Fitz kneels beside me and lays a hand on my back.

The other side is too dark to make anything out but several shapes. "I need more light. It's too dark."

"Use this." I turn and Fitz is holding out a blue glow stick.

"Where'd you get this?"

He pats his arm and says, "Just one of the many things I have stuffed up my sleeve. It's my secret adventure kit. Never know when you're going to need something random."

"Random? Like what? What do you have in there?" I crack the glow stick.

Fitz tugs his sleeve wide near his wrist and peeks inside. "Some beef jerky, a needle and thread, half an Oreo, and this bottle of goop."

My eyes go wide as he pulls out the bottle of goop. It's shimmering black and silver. It reminds me of the black syrup that gave me my magic. "Can I see that?"

"Sure, bro. It's yours," He tosses me the small bottle. I twist the lid and sniff the liquid inside. The black syrup I drank smelled like sour blackberries, this is different. It's more like sweet pickles.

"Do you know what this is for?"

"No clue. Found it hidden inside an adventure book about dragons. There was a note with it, but it was so old it fell apart."

Turning back to the hole, I fling the activated glow stick into the hidden room. It rolls a few feet and then bumps up against one of the shapes. "It's full of broken eggs. Lots of broken eggs..."

"Really?" Fitz asks, butting in towards the hole, trying to get a look. "What kind of eggs?"

"I'm not sure, but they're covered in scales. It can't be..." I trail off, thinking. The small bottle in my hand becomes warm. It can't be. Can it? "We need to get in there. Get back, Fitz. You too, Johnson."

The gnome scrambles away from the hole and back towards the opposite cave wall. The red dog does the same. I glance into the hidden room one more time, shifting myself around to see as much as possible. I don't want any monster surprises. Then I summon up my magic, and say, "Get me inside that room."

The black flies morph into a variety of shovels and pickaxes and start digging out the hole and breaking a path through the wall. The red dog barks from behind me, and I glance back. Fitz is wide-eyed, slowly shaking his head. "Glad you're on my side."

CRACK!

I whip around just in time to see a massive slab of the wall tumble to the ground. My magic swirls and flows back into my hands to wherever they go. I take a tentative step towards the rough doorway and peek inside the hidden room.

Looking left and right, it's clear. I listen hard and only hear the smallest *thump, thump, thump,* which I'm pretty sure is my heart beating in my ears. Fitz steps up beside me. "Whoa, dude, is that… I mean, do you think?"

"I do," I say, stepping into the room and up to the massive pile of eggshells. There must have been hundreds of eggs at one time, but my focus is on the small pedestal in the center of the pile.

It's holding three eggs, each with shimmering black scales. Two are broken—they'll crumble to dust when you touch them. But the other one… the other one is special. It's intact and near its base two black horns shine, having broken through the egg.

I reach down and gently run my hand over the egg. It's warm and alive, but when I try to pick it up, it won't budge. What gives?

"What's wrong?"

"It won't move. It's like it's cemented to the stand." I frown at the dragon egg. I want a dragon, just like Wizard, and here's one—right in front of me. I'm sure of it. But, how do I get it?

"Can you just tell your magic to, like, set it free?" Fitz asks, shrugging. It's not a bad idea, but I doubt that's it.

Magic. Hmm, I wonder.

I lift the small pickle juice bottle and twist off the lid. Holding it up, I swish the syrupy liquid around inside. Then I dump it over the top of the dragon egg.

HISS!

Steam and smoke fill the room. I cough and cover my mouth. Fitz too. The red dog whines. A second or three passes before the smoke clears. The dragon egg looks the same—what happened? That's when I see it. Every so often there's a blip of red from *inside* the egg... like a heartbeat.

"Well?" Fitz asks from behind me.

Reaching down, I easily pick up the dragon egg and hold it in front of my face. Before I know what to do, my magic flows out of me and swirls around the egg. Magic from the egg reaches back, warm against my fingers. Goosebumps run up my arms and down my back.

"It's mine. It's my dragon," I say, as I gently slip it into my bottomless bag. I'm guessing it'll be smart to keep this a secret for now. Shh.

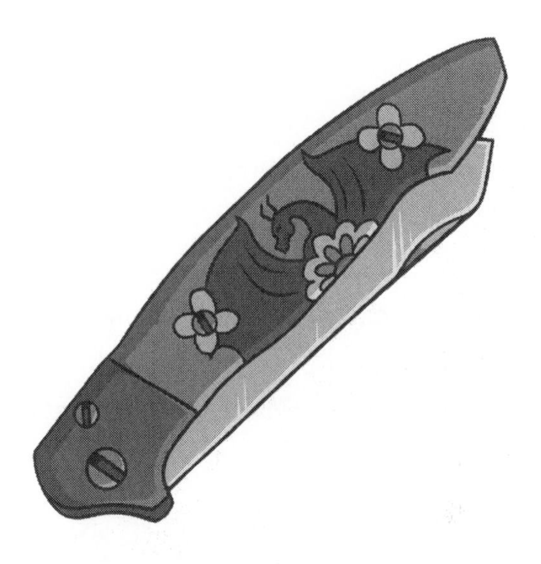

BRENDON'S GIFT

"Dude, I'll wait out here," Fitz says, then slaps his knees and hops around taunting the red dog. "Wanna play, boy?"

Reaching into my bottomless bag, I summon up the tiny dodgeball I tucked away earlier. "Try this," I say, tossing the ball to Fitz. Johnson barks and spins in circles, begging for a throw.

Fitz's eyes light up as he catches the ball. "Hello,

old friend. It's been a long time." He kisses the ball with a loud *pop*.

I don't know.

I look up at a shiny, metal sign flashing with neon lights. Well, half neon lights. There's a cut wire dangling below the dark half, spitting sparks. Flashing on the lit side are messages like "Now for Sale!" and "Hot Shoes" and "Swords that are short." Oh, Grrblin would like this place. The last item on the list is "Sticky Bombs." It's the sign is for *Wendell's Wares*. This is the place.

"Thanks, Fitz. Glad to know you." I smile as I watch him toss the ball for the red dog.

Coming out of the cave maze, he told me about his book project. Being a writer sounds both exciting and weird. One day he's exploring caves, dodging evil robot bugs, and the next day he's staring at a blank wall trying to think of the difference between the words *might* and *may*.

"All good, bro. Glad to be on adventure with you."

I think Fitz may become part of my team. It's always good to have friends around.

I glance at the neon sign again, and it says, "Crossbows? Um, yes!" and "Slingshots." Shaking my head, I open the door and slip through.

Inside there's a single glass case like you'd find in a jewelry shop. It's full of all sorts of gadgets. Most of them shine like metal, but a few are a dull white. Behind the counter is a small door and countless tools hanging on the wall. Maybe they're weapons? I'm not exactly sure. They remind me of the weird tools that Brendon had in his tool bet, only a lot bigger.

"Hello?" I wipe my hands on my jeans. "Anyone here?"

"Finally," Brendon says from my left. Turning, I find him sitting in an old wooden rocking chair picking at his nails with a hooked screwdriver. "Did you get the red dog out safely?"

"He's outside playing fetch with Fitz."

"Who's Fitz—you know what, never mind. I don't care." Standing up, he *clanks* towards me. "I spoke to the witch. She'll talk to you, but only if you bring her a piece of the wild man's beard."

"What? I don't… what?" I feel my forehead scrunch. Hard. I'm going to be stuck here forever.

"It's for one of her potions. I don't know which one."

"Where's this wild man?"

"Easy. It's the big, hairy guy down the street. In the cage," Brendon says, shrugging. "King locked him in there and tossed the key. Some grudge they never worked out."

"How, exactly, am I supposed to get—"

BANG!

The small door slams open and bounces off the wall. "You there! Welcome to my shop. Sorry, didn't hear the door. Who are you?"

It's another gnome. He's wearing red sweatpants and a black leather vest without a shirt. In one hand is a big, rubber mallet. In the other is a can a grape soda.

"That's Wendell," Brendon says, turning to the odd gnome. "Wendell, the kid needs some gear. Help him out, would you?"

"He has coin? I'm not running a charity here." Wendell eyes Brendon, sipping his soda.

"King's account."

Wendell coughs and wipes soda from his nose. Bowing his head, he quickly disappears into the backroom.

"Wait, what's going on?" I say.

"I've got to go. Witch's business, thanks to you. Look, get some gear from Wendell, then deal with the wild man. Use this to find the witch," Brendon says, handing me a rolled piece of paper. I unroll it enough to see it's a map.

"I thought you were going to help me?"

"Kid, I have helped you. Now, you've got to help yourself. Here, take this." Brendon reaches into his tool belt, pulls out a small pocket knife, and slaps it into my hand. Etched into the handle is a small dragon. I unlock and open the blade, then gently brush it with my finger. It's beautiful and sharp.

"What's this for?"

"Pretty much everything. You have knife skills, right?"

"My mom always made me practice." A knot forms in my throat. I slip the pocket knife into my bottomless bag. What will I need knife skills for?

"Good. Get the hair before you visit the witch, or you'll end up something worse than you already are."

"What?" I say, rubbing the back of my neck.

"Go talk to Wendell. Get some gear, you're going to need it," Brendon says, before turning and *clanking* towards the door.

I watch him shuffle out of the shop and wonder what is waiting for me out there? My mind spins, imagining all the possibilities, until an explosion in the back room rocks the shop.

WENDELL'S WARES

I dive to the floor, beneath the glass display case, and cover my head. A flash of light forces me to spin to the right. What was that?

BOOM!

Another explosion from the back. Smaller, but it leaves my head buzzing. What in the world? I start crawling with a single thought. Get to the exit.

WHIR!

Something whirs, then whips past my head. Flipping on my back, I glance around the room. There! Hovering right below the ceiling is a tiny, white disc. It can't be bigger than a quarter. It's spinning so fast, it's glowing red.

"What the…" I say, as the disc burrows through the wall, leaving a smoking hole. Then a golden wand zips out of the hole. It reminds me of one of those honey sticks they sell at grocery stores. What do you think it is?

"Help!" Wendell screams from the backroom. "Kid you out there? Need a little help!"

I tighten my fists and take a deep breath. How do I get to the backdoor? The glass case is blocking everything. I stand up and plant a hand carefully on the edge of the glass. Pressing down, it feels solid. Here goes nothing.

In one quick motion, I vault over the case, landing on the other side in a Stump stance. You know—knees bent, bouncing on the balls of your feet—ready for anything.

HUM! HUM!

I glance over my shoulder to find the honey stick humming as its insides ooze out and form into a raindrop-shaped speaker. Weird. Do you think it has bluetooth?

Inspect programming of tinkered item 455360?

"No time." I turn towards the backroom door. I crouch down to slide through the small door and—

AH-OOH-GA! AH-OOH-GA! AH-OOH-GA!

"AHH!" I slap my hands over my ears and shoulder through the door.

AH-OOH-GA! AH-OOH-GA! AH-OOH-GA!

"Kid, quick! Hit the button on the east wall!" Wendell yells from my right. I whip my head in his direction, and he's just standing there—all stiff like a robot.

"Um, what is going on," I say, frowning.

Wendell's eyes widen, and he snaps his mouth shut as he stretches his head towards the ceiling ever so slightly. Leaning in, I see tiny metal bugs crawling up his neck towards his face. Without opening his mouth, he mumbles, "Button." It sounds like mhm, hmm.

Turning, I see a big red button inside a glass case. What's with all the red buttons here? I dash over and try to find a way to press it, but the glass is in the way. Looking to my right, there's a case of gadgets with a small handful of tools chilling on top. I grab something that looks like a hammer with a triangle top. It'll do. Tap, tap, tap and the glass cracks and crumbles to the floor. I slam my hand on the button.

WHOMP!

There's a flash of light in the room, and I'm hit

by… something. It feels like one of those free-fall rides at the amusement park. My guts zoom into my throat and I keel over, putting my hands on my knees. I think I may be sick.

"Quick thinking using the triangulator, kid. But, uh, next time, use another tool. One more tap and you'd been in big trouble," Wendell says from behind me.

Slowly turning, I glare at Wendell. "I'm going to puke on you."

"Ha. Nice one, kid, here this'll help." The gnome steps closer and flashes a light in my eyes. A cool breeze hits me, then a warm buzz ripples down through my body.

"Whoa." It's like I just ate the best cheeseburger in the world.

"So, what do you need gear for? Are you going on a quest?"

Wendell gets straight to the point. I think I'm on a quest, but I'm not sure what kind of quest. Maybe it's a simple collection quest. You know, go get this, this, and this for me. The first item is a handful of the wild man's hair. But given he's a wild man… this could be something much different.

"Brendon said I need to get a handful of the wild man's beard."

Wendell whistles long and then does a little hop. "Well, let's get you some gear. You're going to need it."

MAGIC ATTACK

DRIVE

THE LEGENDARY MINOTAUR HAS ALWAYS BEEN FAST. BUT WHEN PAIRED WITH THE POWER OF DRIVE? GOOD LUCK. HE'LL SUMMON HIS GO-CART AND CHALLENGE YOU TO A RACE. A RACE THAT'LL ONLY END WITH A FIST TO THE FACE!

MELEE ATTACK

FIST

IT'S ALWAYS THE HORNS THAT HEROES GO FOR. BUT THE MAD MINOTAUR ISN'T GOING TO GORE YOU, NO. HE'LL CORNER YOU AND POP YOU IN THE FACE WITH A FIST. A FIST THAT'LL KNOCK YOU FOR A LOOP. INCOMING WIPE OUT!

FANCY BATTERY

"Kid, there's a small problem I forgot to mention," Wendell says as he looks anywhere but at me.

"Problem?" I lean on the glass case where the triangulator came from. Wendell wanders over and scoops up the other tools, tossing them in a box behind him.

"You got lucky with that triangulator, you know. It's like a hammer, but since the head has three points if you tap, bang, bash—whatever—more than three times, it explodes in your face. But that ain't the problem. A triangulator doesn't need power, most of this gear does." The gnomish engineer slash sales guy waves his hands over the case full of gadgets.

"Isn't there a portable charger or something?"

"There is, it's called a defiberatorionic multi-chamber charge shell, and I'm clean out. Didn't want to tell Brendon, he's got anger—"

I raise my hands and pump the brakes, interrupting. "A battery?"

"Sure, I guess you can call it that."

"I've got one right here." As I slip my hand into my magical jeans pocket, I think about the fancy battery and call it to the top. Grabbing it, I pull it out.

Tinkering Interface Disabled. Power lost.

The message flashes red across my vision, and my Wizard Eyes glow near my eyes. Looking at the glass case and the items inside, everything's different. It's just a bunch of bugs.

"Where'd you get that?" Wendell asks, extra loud.

"Why does everything look like bugs now?"

The gnome clears his throat. "You jacked up your tinkering interface. Can't see the good stuff without it. Put it back, you'll have plenty of juice for any of the gear I have."

Slipping the battery back into my jeans, I get a

power restored message and everything's back to normal. "So, what should I get?"

"What do you want?" The gnome taps the glass case and stares at me.

I peer through the glass. Nothing is labeled, so I have no idea what something is called, let alone what it does. For example: pointy red shoes glisten like they're covered in glitter. Hot shoes, maybe? I inspect them with my Wizard Eyes and get a big fat nothing.

"Are those hot shoes?" I ask.

"Sure are. Put 'em on a witch and if they don't dance around they'll light up like a stovetop. A small heat cylinder in the heel makes them work."

"Okay..."

"Good to stop them from hocus-pocusing you into something. My gut tells me they won't help you. I recommend this." Wendell reaches into the case, pulls out a sticky bomb, and drops it on the case.

"The sticky bomb?" I pick it up. It's lighter than I remember, but otherwise just like Grrblin's version. Picture a whiffle ball with spikes, flickering with light blue flames, and you've got a good idea of what it looks like.

"You know what a sticky bomb is?"

"Sure, but do you have the launcher? The backpack with the tube things," I say, motioning with my hands to show how the tubes run down my arms.

"Interesting, never thought of a launcher. What did you have inside them?"

"Snare or Root. It was the only magic power I had at the time."

"Pfft. Magic. These don't use magic." The gnome grabs the sticky bomb from me, flips it over, and points. "See this dial here? Spin and select the effect you want."

I lean in and see a handful of tiny symbols around it the dial. "What kind of effects?"

Wendell double-checks the symbols. "This one has Smoke, Slick, Sound, Silence, and Symphony. You have a bottomless bag?"

"Yes…" Why is he asking?

"Great." He slaps down a small piece of metal with a red flashing light on its tip—like a matchstick. "Throw this in your bag. After a throw, the sticky bomb will get summoned back to it after a minute, maybe two."

I reach out, take the items, and slip them into my bottomless bag. My Wizard Eyes beep and a new interface pops up in front of me for a gnomish sticky bomb. It's a selection menu for what effect I want to use, each with a description. Nice, that'll be handy.

"What is that," I ask, pointing to a leather collar with silver spikes. It's almost identical to the collar of Wizard's dragon… well, both dragon heads. At one end, a golden latch holds the collar together. Nearby is a tiny keyhole, the shape of a skull.

"That's not for sale."

"Why not, if it's in the case—"

"A King gave that to my great-great-great-times-alot grandfather for safe keeping. Only a King's key can open it, and you ain't got one of those now, do you?" Wendell asks, giving me a sly grin.

"I've seen it before on a two-headed dragon. Does it do anything?" I reach into my jean's pocket and summon my King's key. I want this collar and I have the key to get it. I'm certain.

"Hmm, you've seen more than I'd ever expect. You don't exactly look like the adventuring type, but yes, it's a dragon's collar. It does two things: it allows the dragon's owner to communicate with the dragon and to store a spell in each metal spike."

"A spell?"

"You know… a fireball, a lightning bolt, maybe an ice comet. If you've got the spell, store it in a spike and the dragon can cast it. Just once. It's a one and done type deal."

"Sounds awesome, I'll take it too." I grit my teeth, trying my hardest to keep a straight face.

"Kid, you're not…" Wendell starts to say and lets his thought fall away as I hold up the King's key. The skull glimmers a soft gold, as does the inscription down the haft of the key. “I… I… Okay. You got a dragon hidden in that magic pocket of yours?”

I wink at the gnome as he pulls the collar from the glass case and slides it over. As I slip it into my pocket, another item catches my eye. It’s vibrating and lightly skipping around in the case. I point to the small, silver earbud. It reminds me of headphones. “What is that?”

“That’s a gnomish comms device. I call it—“

“Why’s it dancing around like that? Is it magical?”

“Magical? What are you talking about? It’s not magical. Don’t insult me! That’s one-hundred percent gnomish engineering. Zero magic was used in its construction, there’s no magical nothing.”

“Who can I talk to?”

“Anyone in your group. Your teammates. You formed up?”

I’m not sure if I’m “formed up”. Will this let me talk to my friends? My hands shake, and my face gets hot. If I could talk to my friends… I pick up the earbud, err, the GCD1000—it says so right on the side.

Putting it in my right ear, there’s a whir and I feel it resize and shape to my ear. There’s a crackle and then silence.

“How do I turn it on?” I ask Wendell and he mimes tapping the earbud. I do it and—

“Charlie!” Evie screams into my ear.

GNOMISH TELEPHONE

6

"Noob, what took you so long." It's the good ol' grumpy goblin!

"I miss you guys," I say, sniffling. "Is Stump there, too?"

"He's in the pool," Grrblin says with a chuckle. "He's just about always in the pool."

"The secretary lady waved her hand and a pool appeared. Stump swims a lot," Evie says. I nod my head. I mean, it makes sense. The big man was a shark the entire last level.

"Secretary lady?" Who's Evie talking about?

"The Fate," Grrblin spits out. "Told you we should have stayed out of Fate's business, but, nooo—"

So, it is the Young Lady Fate helping my friends. She's up to something, that's for sure. I wish I knew exactly why she sent me to get help from her sister.

"Kid, get out of my store if you're going to chit-chat. I'll charge King's account for the items," Wendell says, shooing me away and towards the door.

"Items? What'd you get, noob?"

I scoot from the back room and quickly out the door. "A gnomish comms device and an upgraded sticky bomb." I pause. Should I tell them about the dragon collar? I'm not sure if I want anyone to know about the dragon egg yet. But they're my friends… it'll be okay, right?

"Upgraded, eh?"

"It's got six modes I can choose from, and it'll auto-summon back to me after a minute or two."

Grrblin *hmmms* and huffs on the other end. "So, who's the boss there? Or are you on a quest?"

"Maybe a quest to get back?" Evie says, her voice soft and fluffy.

"I'm definitely trying to get back. I'm just not

exactly sure how yet. The 'secretary lady' sent me here to get the help from her sister."

"Sister? What's her name?" Grrblin asks.

"The chef, I guess. I'm trying—"

"Run, and run fast, noob. You don't want anything to do with the chef. That's the worst Fate of all. The numero uno, so to speak. No one's heard about her for a long time."

"Running isn't really an option..." I shrug to myself, wishing it was. "As far as I can figure, she's my only hope in getting out of here."

I hear Grrblin spit and frown. "She's going to make you sign a contract, and that's always, *always* bad news."

I hear Evie squeal in the background and a door slam. Grrblin growls and says something I can't quite make out about a towel. There's a crackle and a familiar voice comes alive in my ear.

"Yo, dude."

"Stump! So good to hear your voice again. How's the pool?"

"It's great. Zombie kid is annoying, though."

"What zombie kid?"

"Tall kid, drones on like a zombie. Always playing this weird arcade game."

"He's playing an arcade game in the pool?" I ask.

"Cabana. In the cabana."

"Oh, in the cabana. Right." I roll my eyes and move on.

"Hey, Charlie," Stump says quietly. "Thanks."

A knot forms in my throat and I squeeze my eyes shut. "Mhm."

"Really. I know what you had to do, and… thanks."

"No problemo," I whisper. It's all I can get out as I rub my eyes. Stump is safe. All my friends are safe. That's all that mattered.

I look around and realize I'm standing in the doorway to Wendell's Wares. Looking down the street to the right, there's a group of people, err gnomes, huddled around something I can't see. To the left is nothing but a big metal wall. Fitz and the red dog are nowhere to be seen. Where'd they go?

"Uh, guys. I have to go. My team is missing…" I say, turning to the right. It's the only way to go. Maybe they're in that crowd somewhere.

"Team?" Evie and Grrblin ask at the same time.

"Kind of. It's this friendly gnome, and oh!" I say a little too loud. "And the ghost dog! It's Johnson! But now he's the red dog—the not dead version of the ghost dog."

"Slow bro," Stump chuckles.

"Anyone make sense of that?" Grrblin says, snickering.

BARK!

I whip my head towards the bark and there's the red dog, standing in the middle of the road. He grins at me, spins in a circle and takes off towards the gnome pile at the end of the street.

"Gotta go!" I yell, sprinting after Johnson. "Stay tuned. I may need help to get out of here."

"Ten-four!" Evie yells and I imagine her skipping around ready for a high-five.

WILD MAN

The red dog dashes through the crowd and I skid to a stop. The throng of gnomes is crowded around a cage, and inside is… the wild man?

"Excuse me." I slip, slide, and shoulder may way towards the man. A few gnomes grunt and bark at me to "watch it." One looks up, her eyes too wide. Quickly, she whispers to another gnome and that gnome to the next and the next and the next. Everyone's looking at me.

"Uh, hi. I'm Charlie." The gnomes bow and clear a path in front of me. As I walk towards the cage, I hear 'King' over and over again.

Wearing King's gear came in handy after all.

The cage is so enormous it could hold a baby elephant, easy. But it's what's inside that I'm focused on. Time for a closer look.

Moving forward, I feel like I'm sneaking up on a sleeping bear. The wild man is huge and has more hair than Mick the Farmer, most of it his enormous beard. I mean, it covers the whole front side of his body. And... you know those tight suits that wrestlers wear? There's one looped around his beard with the slogan 'Be Wild, Be Free' printed across the front.

I don't know.

He's slumped over and snoring, snot bubbles coming out of his nose. Gross. Do you think my ninja-sneak is high enough level to clip a handful of hair for the chef?

The cage bars are pristine and shine like they've never been dirty. Glancing around, I crinkle my forehead. There's no lock on the cage? No door either. Hmm. Tangles of yellow-brown weeds weave in and out of the bars, and in one corner of the cage are bowling balls... with handles?

I don't know.

Near the top of the cage is an odd device. It looks like something out of Wendell's shop. It's rectangle shaped with one side that's slightly rounded. Maybe like an air vent on a jet airplane? It connects to a box secured along the back of the cage with a square, metal tray.

I don't know.

"Fitz, what is that thing?" I whisper, sliding up next to the gnome and pointing to the device. Johnson slips between us and slobbers all over my hand.

"It's an automatic dog feeder, I think. For water, food, possibly snacks. I'd be the saddest writer alive if I never had snacks."

"Why did you guys come down here without me?" The red dog plops onto the ground, his snout resting on his paws, and whines.

The surfer gnome lightly kicks his feet and slumps his head down. "I lost your ball in there..."

I slowly turn my head back to the cage and the wild man inside. Searching around, I don't see the miniature, red dodgeball anywhere. "Where?"

Fitz points right at the wild man.

I tiptoe a few steps forward to get a better view. The ground creaks and the wild man huffs and snuffs, then settles back into his nap. Peering ahead, there's only a ninja move or two more, and I'll be in position to get the hair I need. It's more important than a silly ball anyway.

Slipping my hand into my jeans, I summon the pocket knife from Brendon. Squeezing it in my hand, I crouch into a Stump stance and get ready.

"Charlie," Fitz whispers a bit too loud behind me. "Wait, he's—"

I dive in the air like a long jumper. Squeezing my eyes shut, I whip my feet forward. As soon as I feel the ground, I drop back into the Stump stance to absorb my momentum. Yes! Stuck the landing, soft as a feather.

HRMPH! SNIFF!

A tiny bird twitters and I watch it fly away. Was that in the wild man's beard? I slowly turn around and see the wild man scratching an armpit, a green grin on his face. Ugh. Dude needs a toothbrush. The bearish man turns his head and scans the crowd. "Humph, what y'all want?"

Not moving my head, I glance down. The end of his beard is right there. It's so big, there's no way you'd miss it. Bit by bit, I work my thumbnail into the special spot on the pocket knife, then flick the blade open.

CLICK!

There's a growl inside the cage and my head whips up—the wild man's eyes are fire. Ninja move number two! I whip my free hand down, grab his beard, and yank hard. Surprised, the wild man slams face-first into the ground with a dull *thud*.

"The ball!" Fitz yells nearby. The red dog bark, bark, barks. Out of the corner of my eye, I watch the ball roll across the cage towards the back. There's a low growl, and I look back to the wild man. He's glancing up at me with an evil eye.

I slash the pocket knife down and slice a four-inch length of hair from the wild man's beard.

ROAR!

The wild man bellows like an angry bear and slams a fist into the ground. He pushes himself up. I quickly scramble back, away from the bars and away from the reach of the lunatic.

BARK! BARK!

Johnson appears beside me, yelling at the wild man with all he's got. I wrap my arms around his neck and pull him back. "Easy boy, easy." I keep him out of reach of the giant man's paws.

I notice Fitz slowly making his way to the back of the cage. He makes eye contact and slips a finger across his lips. Shh. Then he starts waving his hands and arms over his head like an orangutan. What the heck? Silently laughing, the surfer gnome sticks out his tongue at the wild man and does the disco fever.

“Dude…” I shake my head. Fitz silent laughs and then reaches for the ball.

The wild man growls, spins around, and slams into the cage bars—flinging Fitz back. The big, hairy man glances around the inside of the cage and then gently picks up the red dodgeball. He turns back to me and holds it up. “This yours?”

THE WILD MAN

MAGIC ATTACK

TAUNT

THE WILD MAN IS ALL ABOUT THE ART OF DISTRACTION. YOU'LL FIND YOURSELF ADMIRING HIS BULGING MUSCLES AND THE BIRD AND BONES IN HIS BEARD, BUT WHILE YOUR TRANSFIXED, HE'S GETTING HIS WAY. AND THAT MEANS YOU LOSING YOURS!

MELEE ATTACK

TOSS

GAMES ARE THE WILD MAN'S WEAPON OF CHOICE. FOOTBALL, BASEBALL, EVEN TENNIS. IF THERE'S A BALL INVOLVED, HE'S BETTER AT IT THAN YOU. BEWARE HIS TOSS, BECAUSE IT'LL KNOCK YOU TO A LAND YOU WON'T REMEMBER! EVER! HA HA!

BAD DEAL

Johnson barks at the wild man, then sinks to his belly and whines as the wild man barks back. "Give it back," I say through gritted teeth.

"Give back my hair."

"I need it."

"You need it? You do not steal a man's beard!" The wild man yells, then quickly calms. Tossing the dodgeball from one big hand to another. "But you're not a man, are you, boy?"

I dig deep into my belly and summon my magic. The black flies swarm out of my hands and into the air. "Circle the cage," I say through gritted teeth.

The wild man watches the magic swirling around him with amusement. "A wizard, eh? I know your type. A man does not fear anything, least of which a wizard."

I send the command and the black magic swarms into the cage. A smile crosses my face as—

BOOM!

The magic blasts from the cage and throws me back to land on my butt. Ugh. Glancing around, the red dog is nearby, along with Fitz, and the wild man is in his cage laughing hysterically.

"What did you do?" I bolt to my feet and storm back to the cage. Careful. Not too close.

"As I said, your magic doesn't scare me. Now, leave me be."

"Give me my ball."

"Unlock the cage first," the wild man says, simply. "I'll give you the ball and let you keep my hair."

"There's not even a lock," Fitz says, piping up, earning a glare from the man in the cage.

"Then I suggest he go look for it under his mother's pillow."

"What are you talking about?" I ask, shaking my head. "My mom's pillow?"

"The answer's there. Steal it and let me out. You get the ball and maybe, just maybe, you'll become a man."

This is getting weird. Do I really need the miniature, red dodgeball? I glance at the red dog and he whines. Johnson, the red dog, the ghost dog—whatever you want to call him, he's saved me time and time again.

I want the ball for him. He's earned it.

Slipping King's key out of my bottomless bag, I feel the weight of it in my hand. Will this open the cage? Even without a lock with a keyhole? It was King who put the wild man in here. I walk to the cage.
"Back up."

The wild man raises his hands like he's surrendering and steps to the rear of the cage.

I wave King's key around, hoping something will happen. Maybe this is like tap-to-pay at the grocery store. My mom always paid with her phone. No card. No problem. I make squinty-eyes at the wild man.

"Not working, eh?" The wild man asks like he knew all along. "Run home to mommy."

Why does he keep talking about my mom? It doesn't make any sense. What does she have to do with anything? She doesn't have a key I could steal, even if… "If I get you out without unlocking the cage, will you still give me the ball?"

The wild man snickers and slams the miniature, red dodgeball into the dirt in the center of the cage. "Show of good faith. It's there for the taking once I'm gone—don't really care how I get out, as long as I'm out."

Dropping Goober's keys back into my pocket, I think of the item I want. This is one of those non-emergency emergencies. I pull out my mom's gold pen and hold it up. Grrblin said it was soul bound, so it should come back to me like it did in Bob's level. I hope so. I really, really hope so.

"You promise not to attack us when you're out?"

He cocks his head to the side and stares at me like he's trying to figure out a math problem. "Look around, I won't attack from anywhere you can see from here," he says loudly. "Beyond that, I make no guarantees."

I look over my shoulder and can still see Wendells, plus a bit more. Do you remember what happened when I used the pen? It cast my one charge of escape for that level and sent my friends back to the beginning of the level. I got left behind (that can happen to the spell's caster). Where the 'beginning of the level' for the wild man is, I have no idea.

But, I'm going to risk it. I have to.

I toss the pen into the cage. The wild man picks up the gold chunk of metal and starts inspecting it. It looks like a toothpick in his hand.

"That's my mom's gold pen. I stole it, and it got me into this mess, now I guess it's going to get you out. Just click the button and—"

HA! HA! HA!

The wild man flops to the ground and goes bonkers! Rolling around in the dirt, he can't stop laughing. "You had it all along, he he. I can't believe it, he he."

In his hysterics, he kicks the red dodgeball near the cage bars, right in front of Fitz. "Fitz!" I yell and point.

The gnome reaches down, snatches the ball out of the cage, and runs over to me. "Got it! Can you, like, bring the pen back before he—"

CLICK! POOF!

"Too late," I say. The wild man's gone, but sparkling on the ground, in the center of the cage, is mom's gold pen. Win, win.

I'll take it.

WITCH'S STEW

"Didn't you look at the map when you got it?" Fitz asks, waving his hands over the map that Brendon gave me. Goober's brother said it'd help me find The Chef, he didn't tell me her shop was right next door to Wendell's.

"No. I saw it was a map about three seconds before Wendell blew himself up," I say, quickly rolling the map and stuffing it in my pocket.

"Wendell blew himself up?"

"I'm pretty sure Wendell blows himself up a lot."

KNOCK! KNOCK!

I bang the door's little metal knocking thing. There's no sign, so I want to avoid barging in, but I'm certain this is the right place... because... the map.

Ugh, Brendon!

"Maybe she's not home," the surfer gnome says, but just then the door creaks open a smidge, and I zip inside.

SLAM!

Fitz and the red dog weren't fast enough. Guess it's just me and The Chef.

"Hello?"

The room is dark and smelly. Like, weird smelly. It's hard to describe. Spaghetti sauce, lemons, and a dash of grass. Sort of, kind of that.

I don't know.

Attached to rough, wooden walls are lit candles dripping lime-colored wax all the way to the floor. Totally a fire hazard.

On the back wall is a massive golden door glittering with ivory dials. Wasn't that behind the throne, where I found the red dog?

In each corner of the room is an enormous, sickly, white tree. The trunk is gnarled and knotty. The knots flicker like they're a blinking eyeball. Long, bare fingers reach up from the tree and slither across the ceiling like snakes.

Front and center is a huge, black cauldron. You've seen them, they're those big pots witches mix nasty things in. It's sitting on a table and the table is littered with oddly shaped knives, twisted roots, and an onion.

BLURP!

Whatever's in the cauldron splutters and bubbles over the lip of the pot, covering the side in rivers of purple-black goop. The ugliest troll I've ever seen wanders up behind the big, black pot. Her skin is a deep army green, freckled in black spots. Two pointy ears peek out of a mop of dark hair. She's wearing a jumbo-sized jumper made from some kind of animal fur.

"Are you—" I start to ask, before she holds up a hand and I snap off my question.

There's a creaking sound and a set of brown teeth appear to float in the air below her big, bulbous nose. Green vapor bellows from her open mouth. I quickly cover my nose as the stench of rotten milk attacks me. Yuck, disgusting.

It's gotta be The Chef.

"Double, double, boil, and bubble. Fire burn and cause some trouble." The Chef scowls at me, then drops something into the pot, and it glows red-hot.

"Yellow, green with some sour cream. In this pot, make some steam."

The Chef's song is deep and scratches at my ears. "Slime of tongue and a twisted root." With two fingers, the witch picks up the weird root from her table and dangles it in front of her face. A black tongue darts from her mouth and slathers the root in spit. She drops it into the bubbling pot with a *plop*.

I'm going to be sick.

As she cackles quietly to herself, she picks up a blade as long as my arm and slices a chunk from the onion. One big *sniff* later, she tosses it into the pot with a splash. "Slice of an onion to make 'em toot."

I reach up and tap my gnomish comms device—twice. There's a click and a crackle as the tech comes alive. Putting my hand over my mouth, I whisper, "Grrblin. Come in, Grrblin."

"What's up, noob? I'm here," Grrblin says from who knows where.

"I'm with The Chef, and she's singing… what do I do?"

My goblin friend laughs. "She's probably casting a spell."

The Chef pauses, eyeing me warily. Grrblin starts to say something else, but I *shh* him quickly. I drop my hand a give the witch a sideways smile.

"Tuft of hair from the wild man. One and only from

this boy's hand," The Chef sing-songs and thrusts out a meaty hand covered in warts.

I reach out to shake the hand. "Uh, hi?"

The Chef smacks my hand away and humphs. Loudly, she says again, "Tuft of hair from the wild man. One and only from this boy's hand."

"Oh, my bad!" I blurt out, reaching into my jean's pocket to grab the wild man's hair. Pulling it out, I drop it into The Chef's hand. She tosses it into the pot of nasty. It sizzles and sings a different kind of song.

"For a portal to avoid trouble. Like an evil to cause toil and trouble," the witch says, briefly pausing to glare at me. She sucks in a deep breath, then wiggles her fingers above the cauldron. Appearing out of nothing, a pause button bobs in the air.

CLICK!

Everything in the big, black pot freezes similar to when Evie paused the game on, uh, the other witch. "Did you just pause—"

"I paused the potion, follow me, Number twenty-two."

"How'd you know to call me that?" I ask, scooting around the frozen pot of sludge to follow The Chef.

"I do speak with my youngest sister. Every so often. She says you need help," she says simply.

The Young Lady Fate is her sister? Thinking back

to everything she told me in the fishbowl, it makes sense. "That makes you…"

"Yes it does. A Fate of too many years." She moves toward a ghost tree in a corner of the room. A plant about as tall as me grows in the shade of the tree. It's ripe with green stalks and weird looking… flowers? Snatching a heavy stalk in one hand, The Chef gently grabs the flowering bulb at the top. It's the size of a small bowl and has layer upon layer of leaves—with thousands of purple needles poking out.

"What is that" I ask.

"An artichoke."

I've eaten artichokes. My mom loves them. You slice the bottom off, and they're full of thorns, cut those out. Then scrape the meat off the bottom of each leaf with your teeth. It's delicious. Even better if you dip them in mayo right before you take a bite. "I've never seen an artichoke like that."

"No? Have you seen one growing before?" The witch asks with a smirk across her face.

"Well, no." I shrug.

"Now you have." She pulls a meat cleaver from a belt tied around her waist. With a quick swipe, she slices just below the artichoke's flowering bulb.

"What's it for?"

The witch whistles and works the knife. "First you slice here and here." She removes the leaves and colorful needles, letting them fall to the floor. "Then you remove the heart. For it's the heart that holds the most flavor—and flavor is magic."

With a flick of her wrist the greenish gray meat splits in two, inside a heart beats soft and slow. She pops it into her mouth, closes her eyes, and makes a *mmm* sound.

"Whoa," I say, as she glows for a split second.

"But, what you need is a needle. To cool the potion."

I bend down and carefully pick up one of the purple artichoke needles from the floor. "Okay, now what? What does the potion do?"

"Ah, we'll get to that. First, we negotiate terms. You don't get anything for nothing, Number twenty-two."

WIZARD'S MISTAKE

"Uh, terms?" I ask, scratching my forehead. "Does this mean you're going to help me?"

"That depends on if we can come to an agreement." The Chef stares at me for a second, then bends down and digs near the base of the three. "Just a moment, it's here somewhere."

"Check, check, come in Charlie. Are you there?"

Evie's voice crackles in my ear as the gnomish comms device lights up.

Turning away from The Chef, I whisper, "I'm here... what's up?"

"Grrblin said to tell you to not sign a contract that doesn't have an escape clause."

I bite my lip and start blinking really fast. "What's an escape clause?"

"No clue, but he said to tell you to figure it out," she says with a sigh. "Then he left for the pool."

"Super-helpful." I roll my eyes. "Tell him I said that."

"Ten-four!"

The troll witch groans and stands up holding a big book. Waving her hand around, a small table appears, and she drops the book on it with a *bang*.

"Do you recognize this book?"

"Um, no?" I'm not sure how I would have seen it before. It's my first time in this room!

"You've read one of it pages, when you stole the playing card from my sister."

"You saw that?"

"I see much. I'm willing to make a deal with you, as I did with Wizard—with a few additional guarantees, that is." The Chef rubs her chin, considering something.

I remember what she's talking about now. I was in Bob's level and saw the young version of Young Lady Fate. In the book, it said Wizard was given the power to change anything in the game in service of the Fates.

"I need to beat Wizard if I'm ever going to beat the game. Your sister thinks I need your help to do that... plus an army." I lower my head and look at my shoes.

"You do need my help, and an army you already have."

"Huh?"

"Your friends. You and your friends can beat him—if you're smart."

My friends. I miss my friends.

"What is a game that no one plays, Charlie?"

I'm not certain how to answer. I scrunch my face so hard I think it's going to crack. "Well, it's a game, I guess."

"Is it?"

"Maybe?" I'm seriously unsure, but if it's not a game, what is it?

"Do you have games at home? Monopoly maybe? Seems everyone has that one, but they never learn a darn thing from it."

"Sure, I've played lots of board games. My grandpa used to ask me to play all the time."

"When was the last time you played?"

"A long time ago." My stomach aches thinking about it. I miss you, Pa.

"I'm guessing those board games are sitting in a closet somewhere. They're just piles of cardboard in a wooden box. This place, this game," The Chef says, waving her hands around and pointing at everything. "It's a *game*. I'm what you'd call a NPC—a non-player character. I'm here to move the game forward for players like you."

"Is the Young Lady Fate a NPC?"

"She is."

"And Lord Rupert? The Dead Horned Rat?"

"Both, yes."

"Wizard?"

"Ah, no. He's a player. A rotten player, yes, but a good one. He made a mistake letting you get to me, though. One which may cost him dearly. But the game needs players. I need players."

"Why?"

"If there are no players, there's no game. So, whether they're good or bad, they serve the game, and me because without them, I do not exist."

"I want to ask about…" I say, my neck hot, sweat dripping from my armpits.

"About your friends?"

I nod my head. "But I don't know that I want the answer." I hold my breath. What if they aren't real?

"Does it matter if they are NPCs too? Does that make them any less your friends? If you only ever played a video game with someone online, can they be your friend? Of course they can. Friends are friends, Charlie."

I relax and feel like I lost a million pounds. I breathe again. That's enough for me. My friends are… my friends.

"Will you help me beat Wizard? You said he was rotten."

"I'll make you the same deal I made him. If you accept, you can change anything in the game, but in return, you will serve me and my sisters—the Fates," The Chef says as she swipes her hand over the big book. My name appears right under Wizard's. The terms of the deal are there… all it needs is my signature.

"What service?" I ask, not sure what that means. "What did Wizard do?"

"He's played the game for a very long time. He brought you here to challenge himself." The witch says, pointing to my Wizard Eyes. "Evie too."

I read the line in the book again. "Let me get this straight. You'll make me as powerful as Wizard, but I can't leave even if I beat the game?"

"Yes and no. If you beat the game, you can go

home. But should Hill House ever be void of players, you'll be summoned here to play another game."

"Is there another way?"

The Chef shakes her head, and I know this is the only chance I have to beat the game, the only chance I have to get back to my friends.

"What would you like to do Number twenty-two?"

MAGIC ATTACK

BREW

DOUBLE, DOUBLE, BOIL, AND BUBBLE IS HOW IT ALWAYS STARTS. BUT HOW IT FINISHES... THAT'S UP TO YOU! FROG, TROG OR GROG. PICK ONE, BUT PAY ATTENTION TO WHAT THE WITCH SAYS OR YOU JUST MAY END UP PART OF THE POTION. HA!

MELEE ATTACK

CLEAVE

SHE MAY PREFER A BREW, NOT ORGANIC AND GLUTEN FREE, RATHER RAW AND RARE. BUT GET ON THE WITCH'S BAD SIDE AND YOU'LL FEEL THE BLADE OF HER MEAT CLEAVER. YOU'LL BE LUCKY TO LOSE A FINGER. OR TWO, MAYBE THREE. HE HE HE HE!

ESCAPE CLAUSE

"Can we add an escape clause?" I ask, remembering what Grrblin was going on about.

"A way to get out of the contract?"

So, that's what an escape clause is. "Yes, exactly." I stand up straight and tall, like I know what I'm talking about.

"Hmm, yes. There's a cereal I want," The Chef says, tapping her chin.

"Cereal? Like that you eat with milk?"

"Yes. I prefer goat's milk."

"I bet Lord Rupert has it. He has everything ever made anywhere."

"Yes, if he's not forgotten where it is," she sighs. "Bring it to me, and you're free from any obligation."

"What's so special about it?"

"It will allow me to leave the game."

Whoa. That's huge. "What's it called?"

"That's for you to figure out."

I frown and The Chef grins before flipping to the back of the big book. She rips out a page and places it on a cutting board. Snatching the cleaver from her belt, the witch makes a quick swipe and *thud* the page is dead—stuck to the board.

I smile wide, trying not to wipe my hands on my jeans.

The Chef writes out the escape clause. A wax seal appearing out of nowhere on the bottom-left of the page—along with the words 'Final and Forever'.

"Sign there." She points to the dotted line, so to speak.

I don't have a pen, but remember what Wizard did the first time I met him.

"Uh…" I hesitate. My heart beats a mile a minute. Should I sign this? I mean, I could be like stuck in this game… forever, right?

"Why the hesitation? You've already signed it once before... this time simply make better choices." The Chef shrugs like it's no big deal.

"Before?" What's she talking about?

The witch waves the question away. "You're already a step ahead with this new escape clause. There's no downside, Number twenty-two. Here—an added bonus."

The Chef yanks on a leather cord around her neck, and a golden key slips out of her jumper. It dangles in front of me, like a carrot on a stick.

"After this key, you need only two more," she says, as I wrap my fingers around the key. The gold is cold and smooth on my fingertips. Quickly, I slip it into my bottomless bag.

Focusing back on the contract, I reach out with a finger, summon my magic, and imagine signing. A small black cloud flows from my finger, swirling this way and that to sign a fancy signature of my name.

The Chef takes a deep breath and then starts to sing. "Double, double, boil, and bubble. Fire burn and cause some trouble."

Waving her hand in the air, the pause button reappears, and she clicks it. The potion in the cauldron flares to life again.

"Wow..." I whisper, my eyes going wide.

"Cool it with a needle of artichoke," she sings,

pointing at me. Me? I point at myself, unsure what to do. "Cool it with a needle of artichoke," she sings again.

"Oh, right." I flick the purple artichoke needle into the potion and there's a quick hiss and then the air gets icy.

"Then start the spell with a shred of smoke." The witch claps her hands and then plops to the ground. "It's ready."

I peek into the black cauldron and there's a dark, gooey mixture inside swirling around and lightly bubbling. "Great. What does it do and how, exactly, do I use it?"

The Chef reaches under her black pot and comes back with a plastic bottle. One like chefs use. It's got a spout on top, use it to squeeze out oil or sauce. She flips it upside-down over the potion and snaps the fingers of her free hand. The potion swirls and then streams into the bottle until it's full.

"Wendell gave you the sticky bomb, yes?" She screws a lid on the bottle and caps the spout. "He should have."

"Uh, yes, but how…" I ask before I shrugging it off, letting the question die.

"Good. Once you're in the throne room, fill it with the potion and set it to smoke. Toss it into a circle, and it'll spawn a portal. There's enough potion for three, maybe four portals."

"Where does the portal go?"

"Home." The Chef tosses me the potion bottle.

I slip the portal potion into my bottomless jean's pocket as The Chef waves her hand. The ivory locks on the massive golden door begin to *whiz and whir*. As they come to rest, there's a *click, click, click* before the door cracks in two and crumbles to dust.

COUGH!

"Ugh, it's in my mouth," a familiar voice says. Once the air clears, there's Fitz and the red dog standing in the entrance of a dark tunnel.

Johnson spins in circles when he sees me and barks like a maniac. Fitz's head is on a swivel as he takes in all the sights. His face bright, just like the first time you tasted ice cream. In his hand is a sword hilt.

"This will lead you back to the throne room. Remember, portals will only open in one of the three circles," The Chef says from behind me.

I've been in the throne room before. Squeezing my eyes shut, I envision it in my mind. Gnomes and angry robots. Ugly trolls. The center white line, two circles...

"Wait, there were only two circles," I say, ticking off everything I remember on my fingers.

"Good luck, Number twenty-two. Be kind to the spiders."

"Spiders?" I turn around to stare at the witch, but the room's empty. No black cauldron, no creepy candles, and no sickly, white trees.

Just the shimmer of the contract I signed, floating in the air like a ghost.

The deal is done.

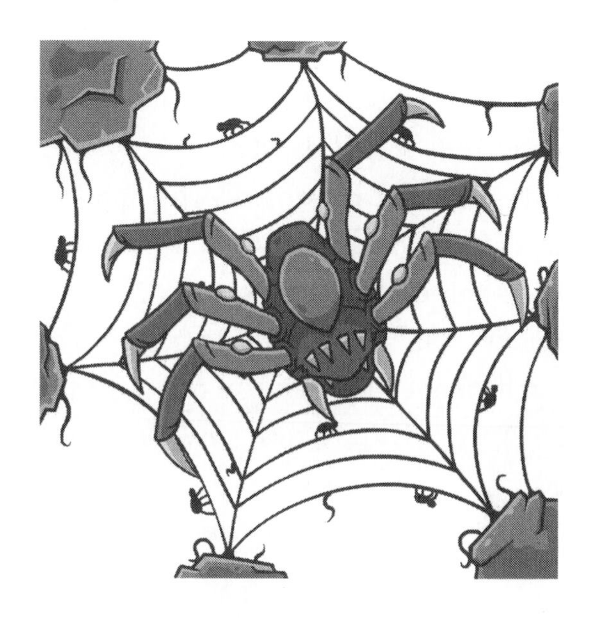

SPIDER STROLL

I turn back to Fitz and the red dog. The silly gnome has a monster grin on his face. "We off on another adventure?"

"Where there's a dark tunnel, there's adventure." I laugh. "Did you hear what the witch said?"

Fitz tilts his head to the side. "Witch? No..."

I point at the dark tunnel behind him. "We need to get to the other side, but it's full of spiders."

The blood drains from the surfer gnome's face and his eyes go wide. Slowly, he turns around and peers into the tunnel. The red dog whimpers, scampering behind the gnome. "I'm a writer, I write things. Adventures, monsters, fantastical things," Fitz whispers to himself, between short, quick breaths.

I stroll up, join him and Johnson, and get a good look into the tunnel. "It's the cave maze. Isn't it?"

"I'm a writer, I write things. Adventures, monsters, fantastical—"

"Dude, snap out of it." I bop the tiny gnome on the head.

Fitz shakes his head and there's a rattle. "Careful with the equipment. Writers ain't rich, you know." He slips off his winter hat. Nestled inside is the miniature, red dodgeball. Gently lifting it out, he inspects the wires and gears of his automatic writing device.

I grimace and sharply suck in a breath. "My bad, all good?"

He nods, slips the ball back inside, and eases the hat back on his head. "I've only been through the cave maze with the string. This must be another path, hopefully not *the best way*."

"It goes to the throne room. Maybe it's a straight shot. We'll pop out in the right spot, I'd bet on it."

"What's there?"

"It's where I can open a portal to go home. I—" I pause. Where's Fitz going to go? I assumed the red dog would come with me, but never considered the gnome. "—do you want to come? It'll be an epic adventure."

"How epic?"

"Final boss, epic."

"Right on! I'm in, for sure," the excited gnome says, a huge grin on his face. "Oh! Here. Wendell said this was for you." He tosses me the sword hilt I saw earlier.

The handle is black metal wire wrapped tight. It's got great grip. The actual guard is a single bar of dark silver metal capped with a clockwork gear on one side and a sprocket on the other. Hmm, I wonder. Summoning my magic, I imagine the sword in my hand. Blade and all.

WHOOSH!

Magic explodes from the hilt into a sword, much like Mr. Pointy—it might as well be a black-bladed lightsaber. Nice!

I swish the blade through the air, testing it out. I feel a grin crawl across my face. "Let's go. Leave the spiders to me."

One step into the cave maze and there's a *click, click, click* up ahead. Johnson whines, snuggling up close to my leg. I reach down and give him a pat.

Deeper in the tunnel, tiny lights twinkle here and there—weaving a web of sharp red light between the cave walls. *Click, click, click,* and the lights slip and fade everywhere and nowhere all together. They're spider eyes. Creepy.

"Spiders…" Fitz whispers.

A spider scurries towards us and I drop into a Stump stance. Bouncing on the balls of my feet, wide and solid. I brandish my clockwork blade like a shield. There's no loosey goosey here, I'm ready for anything. "Easy, easy…"

Four red lights, *ting, ting,* as the spider blinks its triangle shaped eyes. Below them are ferocious looking fangs the size of my hand. I gulp, hard. It's made of metal, like everything else in this level. *Click, click, click,* and it darts to my left on too many silver legs.

BARK!

Johnson hops forward a step, between me and the robot. The spider rears back. Its front legs *shing* up like knives. The red dog takes the warning and scampers back, out of range.

BARK! BARK!

The spider doesn't move to attack. It dances further back. Simply watching the barking dog. Interesting.

"Whoa, easy boy," I say, calming Johnson down. Inspecting the spider, my Wizard Eyes say it's a silver spider. That's it. Great, super-helpful.

The silver spider spins and scurries away to join the others. "Why didn't he attack? Are they nice spiders?" Fitz asks in my ear. Is there such a thing as a nice spider?

"Fitz stay close. You too." I look at the red dog. They snuggle up to me. "Okay, not *that* close."

Slowly moving forward, more spiders come into view. The tiny, red eyes blink as we pass. My clockwork blade, always out front. One, two, three... there are countless spiders. Turning a bend, there's a light up ahead and plenty of green. What the... I squint to see better. Is that a field?

"Charlie..."

"Stay close. Move with me." I turn and walk backwards—careful to keep my blade up and ready for trouble. "Nice and slow."

The tunnel gets brighter and brighter from whatever is up ahead. The spiders move as we do, but don't attack. I step, they step. It's a weird dance, but I'll take it.

A bitter smell bombards my nose, and I'm reminded of lawn mowers and cut grass. Glancing over my shoulder, it's a field. Did we miss a turn?

There's a bright flash in the center of the field. A big, hairy, hulking figure steps out of the light into the grass. Locking eyes with me, he grins and rushes forward.

"It's him!" Fitz shouts in my ear, forcing me to cringe.

"Ain't no cage in sight, boy!" The wild man yells and then bellows with laughter.

CLINK!

"Back, back into the tunnel" I move quickly.

"Dude, stop," my gnome friend says, grabbing my shoulder. I look at him, and he nudges his chin towards the tunnel we just came out of.

"What the..." There's a super-sized spider web blocking the way!

I peek away for two seconds and now a spider web the size of a car? The silver spider sits on top of the web, and billions of smaller spiders swing from sticky threads of web.

Whipping around, the wild man growls and barrels straight at me. "Never cut a man's beard. You're mine now!"

I freeze, and my mind goes blank.

"Charlie!" Fitz yells, shaking me until I snap out of it. "Look at what's in his hand."

"Is that a dodgeball?"

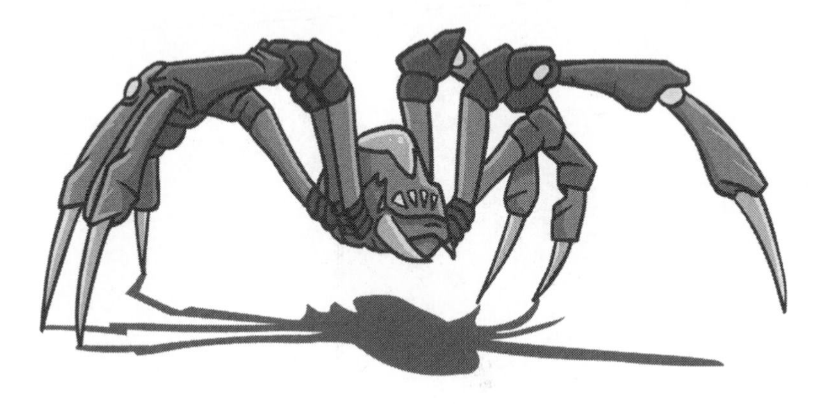

MAGIC ATTACK

WEB

WEBS ARE THE MASTERWORK OF SPIDERS. THE SILVER SPIDER INCLUDED. BUT HER WEBS ARE BOTH BEAUTIFUL AND DEADLY. THREAD BY THREAD THEY'RE SPUN SILENTLY AT SPEED. ONE SECOND YOU'RE FREE TO GO, THE NEXT IT'S A BIG FAT NO. HA!

MELEE ATTACK

SILENCE

THE SILVER SPIDER WILL LEAD YOU WHERE SHE WANTS YOU TO GO. GUIDING YOU THROUGH THE DARK WITHOUT A SOUND. IT'S NOT WHAT YOU SEE THAT'S DEADLY, IT'S THE SILENT SPINNING OF HER WEB THAT'LL TIE YOU IN KNOTS. FOREVER!

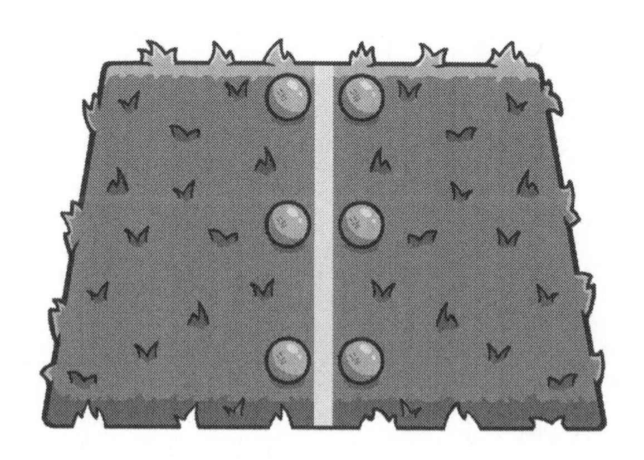

DODGE BALL

The wild man skids to a stop in front of me, huffing and puffing, like, well, a wild man. "Put your sword away, boy."

Glancing to Fitz and back to the crazy eyed man in front of me, I raise my clockwork blade like a shield. "I think this is better."

"Bah. Put it away. We're going to settle this like men."

"By playing dodgeball?" I raise an eyebrow and point at the bright red ball in his hand. "Are you kidding?"

"Yes, dodgeball. Games are the great equalizer." He slaps the dodgeball with his free hand. It echoes a rubbery *crack*.

I open my mouth once and nothing comes out.

Hmm. I wonder.

Opening it a second time, a question pops out. "What are the rules?"

The wild man reaches down and taps the ground with a meaty finger. Instantly, a bright, white line about as wide as my hand appears and shoots across the field. As the line draws itself, the illusion of the field dies.

The grass turns to a cold metal floor. Ugly trolls crowd around a white-lined circle to my right. Noisy robots *clink, clank* in a circle on my left. Their gnome engineers nearby, tools at the ready. Straight ahead is the mountain of gym shorts where I met Brendon. You can smell it from here.

"Whoa," Fitz whispers and I turn around.

He's peering into the hole Johnson tore in the purple throne. The stuffing and springs still exposed. Behind the throne is the spider web wall, closing a gaping hole in the golden door with the ivory locks. Where'd the tunnel go?

Everything begins to flicker like there's a bad internet connection. Suddenly, The Chef busts through the door, her hand spinning the ivory dials one by one. A dragon with a spiked collar appears behind the purple throne. Its shimmering black claws grip the ornate chair as it grins at me.

"Uh, Fitz. Was that real?" I ask, as it all disappears, leaving nothing but Fitz with his head down the hole of the torn up throne.

"Was what real?" Fitz asks, his head popping up.

"Boy! Choose your side," the wild man shouts from behind me.

Turning around, I see different colored dodgeballs appear along the center white line. On one side are the ugly, green trolls sporting dodgeball t-shirts and sharp swords. On the other are gnome engineers and their robots. One of the gnomes gives me a quick wink and I jog over to join them. Fitz right behind me. Where's the red dog?

"Turn-based attacks only. You—"

"Turn-based?" Fitz asks, interrupting.

"He throws," the wild man says, pointing at me. "Then you throw, then when you've both missed by a mile, I'll throw."

"That's not dodgeball," I say a little too loud. "If we're going to play dodgeball, let's play dodgeball."

The wild man growls and stares straight at me

without looking away, for like ever. My armpits sweat and… is it hot in here?

"Fine. I get hit, you win. I catch it, you lose," the wild man says.

"That's—"

"Your only other option."

I glare at the big hairy beast. Fitz gently places his hand on my shoulder and I turn. "It'll be okay, we can do this." There's a mischievous grin on his face.

Does it even matter? I mean, all I need is to distract him long enough to open a portal, then hop through. How hard could that be?

"Agreed," I say, and the wild man turns, stomping to the center of the field. Letting go of my magic, I slip the clockwork blade's hilt into my bottomless bag. Next, I pull out the sticky bomb from Wendell and the portal potion from The Chef.

"Do you have a plan?" Fitz asks, taking off his hat and grabbing the miniature, red dodgeball. I totally forgot about that thing!

BEEP!

I spin and look for the sound. Above me, a scoreboard slides down from the ceiling.

BEEP!

A countdown timer ticks down from 7… 6… 5…

BEEP!

3… 2… 1…

A voice straight out of a video game says, "Combatants, fight."

"GAME ON!" Fitz screams and hurls the tiny, red dodgeball across the field. It's a heat seeking missile, and its target is the wild man.

"AHH!" The wild man screams, diving to his right, tumbling through a group of trolls like a bowling ball.

"Dude..." My eyes going wide, and my mouth drops open. "That was... dude, that was awesome!"

Fitz shrugs. "Still missed."

"But it was a rocket. If I—"

"Dive!" The friendly gnome shouts. I don't hesitate and nosedive to my left.

WHOOSH!

Wind ruffles my hair. I just see the red *thing* zipping past my face. Scrambling to my feet, I take in the field. Every troll and robot is on the move. It's chaos as each side tears up the floor trying to get a dodgeball.

Fitz takes off, away from me, and snatches up three balls in one go. He launches them like a madman and an entire pack of trolls goes down. He punches the air and shouts in victory.

Think, Charlie, think.

Calling up the sticky bomb menu in my Wizard Eyes, I scroll through the options. Choosing Slick, the baseball sized item in my hand gets heavier as it fills with something. I rip my arm back and hurl the sticky bomb across the field towards the wild man.

He dodges with a quick hop to the side. The sticky bomb crashes into the metal floor, but doesn't break open. Rather, it slides forward in a circular motion, stopping right below the wild man. "Ha! You throw like a two-year-old. Nice miss."

"Was it though?" I yell across the line. The wild man eyes flash, and he glances to the side. There's a faint *click*. The sticky bomb snaps in two and spills out a black liquid. Do you think it's oil?

I don't wait to see what happens next. Sprinting across the field, I weave through gnome engineers and mean-looking robots. They're not paying attention to me, but rather fighting off the trolls with some kind of gadget. I double-take. It's a dodgeball rocket. Nice!

Dashing to the right around a dogbot, I see the circle. As I get closer, I feel my sticky bomb drop into my bottomless bag. The automatic-summon feature is a game-changer. I quickly rip it out and switch to Smoke mode, like the witch said to do. I fill it with portal potion.

"Fitz! To me! To me! Johnson! Here, boy!" I quickly swivel my head and glance around the field, I don't see either of them. Where are they?

ZIP! ZIP!

Multiple dodgeballs zip pass my head and bounce

away behind me. Faster. I must be faster. Getting lucky is *not* an option. I toss the sticky bomb into the white circle, and it clanks on the ground.

VZZZZT!

Splitting the sticky bomb in two, a square portal opens and shimmers like a shimmer door. My Wizard Eyes flash red and a message appears. *Portal inactive. Activate paired portal to activate.*

I shake my head. Ugh. Do what?

"Boy! I'm coming for you," the wild man shouts, and I spin. He's rushing the center line—hands, arms, and beard full of dodgeballs. Out of the corner of my eye, Fitz, and the red dog, dash towards me. The friendly, surfer gnome has an orange dodgeball locked and loaded.

I rip the sticky bomb from my bottomless bag again (it already came back) and fill it with portal potion. Sprinting past Fitz, I circle a dogbot and look for the white circle on the troll's side of the room. Where is it? I can't see anything but an extra-large circle of trolls. They're clutching dodgeballs, but not making any moves.

A gnome engineer runs up and tugs on my arm. "Gotta high-toss," he says, mimicking what he means. "Over their heads."

"Thanks!" I bring my arm down for an underhand throw and launch the sticky bomb and portal potion into the air. As it floats towards the guarded circle, the trolls launch their balls at the sticky bomb, trying to knock it off its path.

BANG!

One catches it and launches the potion off course. It slams into a dogbot. The robot shakes and squirms, falling to the ground like he's out of commission. Dashing over and snatching up the sticky bomb, I refill. I also summon my magic, but not for a sword or a direct attack.

With one hand grasping the refilled sticky bomb, and the other hand a ball of magic, I scoop low and make an underhand toss.

"Catch this!" Fitz screams. I turn in time to see him launch another missile at the wild man. It cracks the big fuzzball in the head and bounces high in the air.

"Ball! Ball!" The wild man shouts, pointing at the ball flying through the air. "Someone catch it!"

Quickly, I glance back to watch my ball-o-magic sail through the air. The troll guards shoot rockets into the sky to knock it off the path, but that's okay. I drop my elbow and make a sidearm throw low to the ground and send the sticky bomb skidding across the floor.

It zooms right past the feet of the trolls and into the second white circle.

VZZZZT!

The second portal opens. *Portals active. Single-use only.*

Single-use only?

BOOM!

"AHH!" Fitz shouts as a boom vibrates through the playing field. I whip towards him and see a dodgeball the size of the wild man bouncing away and Fitz flying in the air—right for the open portal.

"Fitz!" I dash towards him, but know it's too late. He flies right into the portal, and it *zips* closed. Fitz is gone. The red dog barks and whines at the spot where the gnome disappeared.

Is the other portal still open? I turn, and it's there, but how do I get there?

"Charlie!"

I whip around towards Fitz's voice, and he's on the other side of the field! How could I have missed that? A portal pair. It's only going to take him from one spot to the other. I rack my brain.

The Chef said there were three circles. But I've only ever seen two. I scan the field, desperately searching for the other circle.

BARK!

The red dog takes off. Where's he going? I turn and see him making for the mountain of gym clothes sitting in a circle on the floor at the edge of the field.

Hmm. I wonder.

I snatch the sticky bomb out of my bottomless bag and refill it with portal potion, one last time. This is it. I'm out of potion, so if I'm wrong. I'm in big trouble. Sprinting like my life depends on it (because it does) I catch Johnson. He's chomping on a pair of dirty gym shorts. Gross.

Kicking a pair out of the way, I see it. A white line. Yes! I drop the sticky bomb right there.

VZZZZT!

A golden portal opens and shimmers, on the other side I barely make out where it goes. Home.

Final portal active. Single-use only.

My stomach drops. My heart jumps into my throat. I turn back to Fitz and the red dog. I can't leave them.

"Go, dude!" Fitz shouts as he barrels towards the wild man. "Bestseller, man!"

I can't help but smile.

Looking down, there's Johnson. The red dog. "Hey boy. I'm sorry." I rub his fur, right between his pointy ears, like he likes it. He nudges my hand towards the portal. It's like he's saying to go. Like he knows it'll be okay. I take the whistle from around my neck and slip it around the red dog's neck. "Maybe you and Fitz will make it through another way."

I stand up, then jump through the portal.

HOME ALONE

Home.

I'm really here.

The door jamb is busted and paint is peeling from the wall.

The smell of meatloaf wafts through a crack in the window.

It's probably vegan.

Peeking through the window, she's inside. Dancing. Singing.

"I'm sorry, Mom."

I peel the Wizard Eyes off my face, and let them dangle in my hand.

Shrugging, the weight of my backpack is there. It's a heavy reminder. The portal must have reset everything.

"I'm sorry, Mom," I whisper one more time.

I'm not done yet. The game's not over.

Turning away from my front door, I see the trail that leads up the mountain. Evie found it the first time. We went to Hill House together.

This time, it's just me. But that's okay. I'll see my friends soon enough.

I start to run.

I can't get back soon enough.

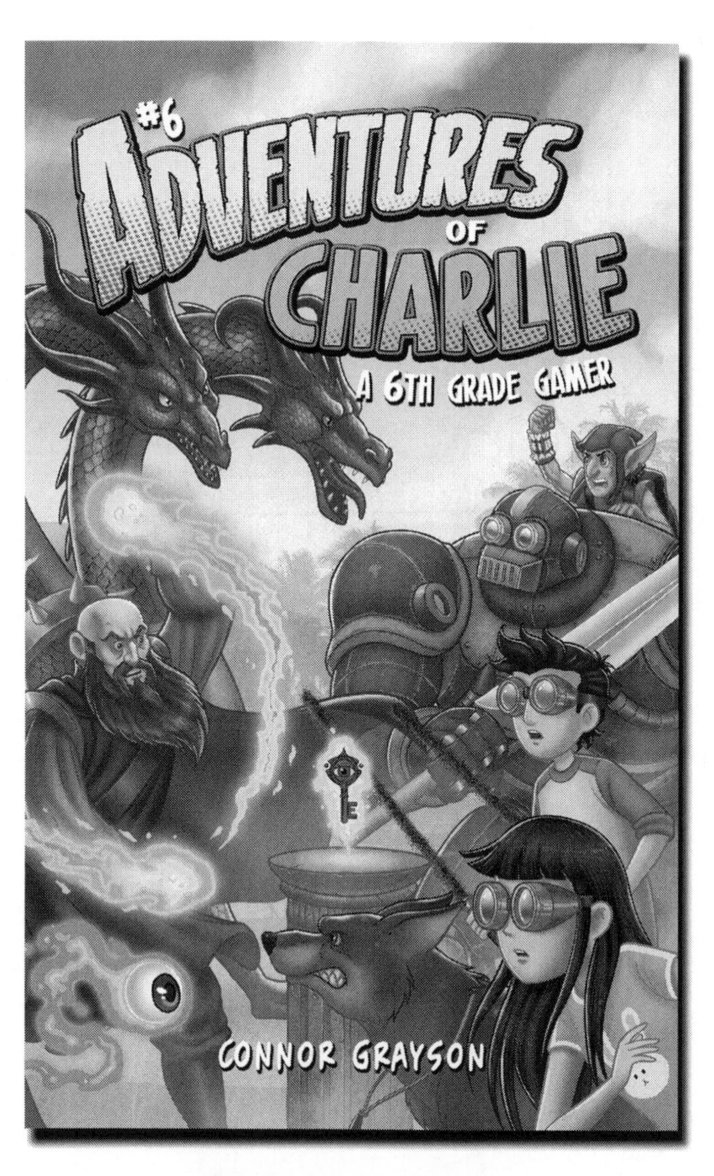

BOOK #6

THE ADVENTURES CONTINUE!

FOLLOW ME AT 👇

CONNORGRAYSON.COM

- Just like Charlie, meatloaf is my favorite food. My mom always slathered a mix of ketchup and brown sugar on top. 😋
- In 6th grade, my friends and I challenged the girls volleyball team to a game. We lost. 🏐
- In 5th grade, my dad bought the first family computer. It looked like two huge white boxes. A company named Tandy made it. 🖥
- When I was 11 years old I had a hound dog. We'd walk at night. Sometimes he would get scared, press his head up against my knee, and whine. 🐕

If you liked this book, please **leave a review for it.** I'd appreciate it, because it helps other readers find books they may like. Thanks!

Made in the USA
Las Vegas, NV
20 February 2023

67832234R00079